THE DISCIPLE

SARAH SHERIDAN

BLOODHOUND
— BOOKS —

Print ISBN 978-1-913942-47-2

ALSO BY SARAH SHERIDAN

The Convent

For my three superstars, Bethan, Olivia and Ben

1
_____

Five days before the catastrophe, Sister Veronica pulled her old shawl tightly round her shoulders as she stomped down the staircase in the Convent of the Christian Heart. Great Heavens, it was chilly. She would have to knit a thicker cloak at this rate. She stopped for a minute and stared through the hall window at the bronze leaves swirling around London's Soho Square gardens. The weather, she reflected, was making it clear that following the infliction of a scorching summer, it was gearing up for an unpleasant onslaught of freezing autumn winds. And Sister Julia Augusta, her formidable Mother Superior – who was always one for a spot of mild suffering – had stated with resolution that their heating was not to be turned on until at least October. Sister Veronica tutted under her breath, wondering if the nation would ever again hear the word 'mild' during a weather forecast. She would have to find Sister Agnes an electric radiator for her bedroom or her arthritic pain would get even worse during these September days, and she couldn't stand seeing the agony in her friend's face as she tried to kneel in chapel. And to think, two weeks before they'd all been fanning themselves in the convent garden, talking about how sweltering it was.

Hearing a gurgle from the kitchen, an indulgent smile broke across her face and she made great effort to increase her stride, ignoring the itching on her legs from her new tweed skirt. It was such a treat to have a baby in the building. Even if the cause of the little one's arrival was so disturbing. For a moment, mental pain stabbed at Sister Veronica; the scars in her mind caused by poor Jamie Markham's murder still fresh and unhealed. Flashbacks of her abduction – a result of her investigative efforts into justice for Jamie – tormented her daily. She'd been in hospital, of course, recovering from the whole ordeal, *and* a broken arm, Saints preserve her – only recently out of plaster – when Agnes had visited and announced that an infant had been abandoned on the doorstep of their convent. Sister Veronica suspected her sly old friend had used this news as a means to jog her back to reality, to some sort of sense of self, knowing she was far too curious a person not to be interested in the baby's arrival. Especially when the only two items left with the baby – one enigmatic and one horribly sinister – were taken into account.

And the baby is who matters now, Veronica, she told herself. *Stop ruminating on the past and immerse yourself in the present. We'll have none of that morbid thinking today, thank you very much. There's too much work to be done. Dearie me, pull yourself together, old girl.* Shaking her head slightly, trying to dislodge her dark thoughts, she marched down the hall and entered the kitchen, a huge beam immediately illuminating her face.

'Great Saints, Veronica, I'm so glad you're here.' Sister Catherine was holding the baby girl out in front of her as though she were an active bomb. An unmistakeable stink of dirty nappy pervaded the room. Teething toys lay haphazardly across the nun's knees and floor, and a high chair stood like a throne next to the wooden table, its tray covered in pea-green puree. Taking note of the grey bags under her friend's tired eyes, and the fact that the nun's shirt buttons were all in the wrong holes, Sister Veronica immediately took the wriggling child from her, hugging her close.

'Go and have a rest, Catherine, you look exhausted. I'll take care of Hope for a while, she can help me with my errands this morning.' The Sisters at the convent had agreed on the temporary name of Hope for the baby the week before, believing it signalled great confidence in them eventually finding the child's mother, as well as a general positivity for her future. And, of course, St Paul had written about the importance of hope to the Corinthians, as Sister Irene had piously pointed out. But the Bible verse was no longer of such importance from Sister Veronica's own perspective, since her belief in the Roman Catholic Church had been rocked to its core during the tragedy of Jamie's murder and its aftermath. Still working on her own sense of personal faith, she was aware that she was turning into somewhat of a rebel nun, but that was absolutely fine with her.

'Oh thank you, Veronica.' Sister Catherine – whose claims that she didn't have a maternal bone in her body were becoming increasingly frequent this week – reached for a baby wipe and cleaned a splodge of baby food from her shoulder. 'I managed a few bits of broken sleep last night, but Hope was determined that I shouldn't shut my eyes for more than forty-five minutes at a time. I can hardly think straight, I'm so drained.' She glared at the baby, who was now craning her head back, giving Sister Veronica a gummy grin. 'She's a sleep terrorist.'

'Now then, Catherine, off you go to bed,' Sister Veronica said, motioning for her to get up. She smiled back at the baby, a rush of love and delight consuming her. 'Hope and I will be absolutely fine, don't you worry about a thing.' Sister Catherine patted her friend's back appreciatively as she staggered from the room.

Taking the child straight to the bathroom, where the nuns had enjoyed installing a fully stocked changing table shortly after the baby's arrival, Sister Veronica reflected that it was rather amusing that the note left with Hope had said, *Take me to Sister Catherine*. The universe, she thought, had a habit of pairing the most unlikely people together, often two complete opposites who tended to rub each other up the wrong way. It was either a cosmic joke, she decided, or an opportunity for reluctant personal understanding.

Most of the nuns had welcomed the baby into their lives with open arms, apart from Sister Irene, of course, who had said it was inappropriate for the baby to stay, and that she should be put in foster care. But police had taken DNA from Hope, and found from their database that her mother was Mona Adkins, a working girl in Soho and – surprisingly – a distant relative of Sister Catherine. Sister Catherine had arrived at the convent from Australia eighteen months previously, but her family originally hailed from the UK, and as she'd admitted herself, surprising long-lost relatives kept popping up all over the place. Social services said that as long as Sister Catherine was happy to look after the baby, they would release the infant into her custody temporarily while they continued to work on the case. Persuaded to agree to this by a cluster of overjoyed nuns, Sister Catherine had nervously consented.

Of all the nuns at the convent, Sister Veronica mused, Catherine was the least interested in children and had always seemed rather intimidated by their need for constant upkeep and attention. Care for the baby was shared willingly among everyone there, but Sister Catherine, being the child's relative, did most of the night-time formula feeds and was now clearly struggling. Her usually ruddy face was grey and haggard, and she'd begun to do strange things. During supper the day before she'd poured salt into her tea instead of sugar, and the day before that had put the butter away in the freezer instead of the fridge. It had taken a whole day to defrost, much to Sister Irene's very vocal chagrin. Hmm, if only she could take Hope away for a bit and give her poor friend a rest. And it would be lovely to spend more time with the baby, who she'd felt an immediate, strong bond with.

'Now, now, don't get too attached,' Sister Veronica muttered under her breath as she wrestled another baby wipe from the packet. 'Hope needs a proper family, one way or another, best thing for her. She can't carry on living in this musty old convent forever, goodness gracious that would never do.' She knew she needed to step up her search for Mona Adkins, she'd been too lax the last few days, spent too much time showing the baby around the garden, reading her books and swaying her to sleep. She was enjoying her a bit too much, she felt. And putting off the inevitable time when she'd have to say goodbye to her. She had started to look for Mona, of course, putting feelers out here and there in the local community and chatting to some of the local working girls, who'd just yesterday given her an address of Mona's friend, Crystal. She was planning on visiting the girl later that day and using a softly-softly approach to find out if she knew anything. But the truth was that her initial searches suggested Mona had seemingly disappeared off the face of the earth.

'Aren't you a good girl,' Sister Veronica said absent-mindedly, as she snapped a row of Babygro poppers into place over the freshly applied nappy, the soft material immediately coming together to cover the island-shaped birthmark on the baby's thigh. Hope wriggled enthusiastically. As she stood up straight, cursing the old bones in her back that had begun to ache, Sister Veronica caught sight of herself in the small bathroom mirror.

Extra lines and wrinkles had appeared all over her face since the Jamie Markham affair. Those didn't bother her, but the haunted look in her eyes did.

'We both need to get away,' she said firmly, picking Hope up. A wet gurgle was the reply. 'I need a holiday and you need to give poor tired Sister Catherine a break; shame on you for keeping her up at night, my dear. But goodness knows how we are going to manage that; Mother Superior says she wants to keep a close eye on me after what happened last time, more's the pity. Right, come on, young lady, we need to go and visit a nice girl called Crystal who works near here. Although will she be awake?' She paused. 'By all accounts, she tends to conduct her business after dark. Oh well, we'll keep knocking until she answers.'

Twenty minutes later, Hope, sporting a new pink coat and hat proudly purchased the day before by Sister Pemii, was cosily ensconced in the pram that had been kindly donated to the convent by a parishioner. Full after some warm milk, her eyelids drooped. News of the baby's arrival had spread fast through the local Catholic community and many more visitors than usual dropped by the convent each day, hoping to get a cuddle with the new arrival; with lots of them donating bundles of second-hand clothes and toys. It was amazing how an unexpected situation brought out the kindness in some people, Sister Veronica had reflected many times since, grateful for the huge collection of toys, play mats, clothes and other apparel that she had previously no idea modern babies needed. She'd had three possessions as a young girl; a toy lamb, a Bible and a china doll that her mother never let her play with in case it broke. Hope already had enough playthings with which to open a shop and she was still so young she couldn't even hold or use half of them.

Before Sister Veronica could lug the heavy pram through the

front door and out into the biting air, the sour face of Sister Irene appeared in front of hers.

'Taking the baby out *again*, I see?' Sister Veronica often marvelled at Sister Irene's ability to make every sentence she uttered sound condescending.

'Yes, that does appear to be the case, when you consider that I'm attempting to push the pram out of the front door,' Sister Veronica replied. 'Now excuse me, Irene, I have things to do.'

'I just wanted to let you know that I've lodged a complaint with social services about the baby staying here indefinitely,' Sister Irene said, her thin mouth twisting into a grimace. 'I can't stand her constant babbling and crying at night; it's stopping me from sleeping. And you know how I need my rest, Veronica.'

Sister Veronica inflicted her most withering gaze on Sister Irene.

'Can't you just enjoy the fact that we have this beautiful four-month-old girl with us, Irene? She's a relatively easy baby, by all accounts. I feel it is a gift from God that we are allowed to look after her at this time.'

'No, I cannot "just enjoy" her being here, Sister. She's distracting some of the other Sisters from their duties. Sister Catherine was apparently *unable* to come to chapel the other day because she was too busy looking after this small human being. So I have petitioned social services to remove the child from our custody and place her somewhere else.'

'How very charitable of you, Sister.' Sister Veronica's tone was icy. 'And how very unsurprising. Now I'm going out, so excuse me.' As she rammed the pram past the thin nun's body, she caught sight of the other object that had been left with the baby. A tarot card, depicting an awful image of chaos, fire and death, with the word *Destruction* inscribed in Gothic letters across the bottom. Mother Superior had placed the card on the hall shelf, perhaps so the nuns didn't get too comfortable with

Hope and forget about the circumstances of the baby's arrival. The sight of it always sent a cold shiver through Sister Veronica. The contrast between the sinister implications of it, and the beautiful, pure baby girl in their safe keeping was too much to bear. What kind of person would do that – leave such a terrible tarot card on top of an innocent infant? And more to the point, why?

Reprimanding herself for being pleased that she'd left Sister Irene wincing and rubbing her leg – the pram did have such sturdy wheel arches after all – Sister Veronica marched proudly across Soho Square, enjoying the smiles she and the now sleeping Hope were receiving from passers-by.

Turning away from the leafy greenery of the square, and down increasingly seedier streets, Sister Veronica navigated the pram through beer bottles, kebab debris and cigarette butts until she reached a shabby, pale-yellow door. Above it was a neon sign spelling out *Girls, Girls, Girls* that looked rather pathetic in the daylight. By night it no doubt lit up in red, guiding prospective punters to the girls' rooms.

Suddenly wary about the reception she'd get after announcing her arrival, Sister Veronica paused. Usually so bloody-minded, she felt apprehensive about knocking on the brothel door. But then again, what choice did she have? The police weren't telling Sister Catherine anything about their investigation into the whereabouts of Hope's mother, Mona. And round here they certainly had bigger problems to deal with; every night was punctured by wailing sirens in this part of London. Moreover, she had a feeling that Sister Catherine wasn't telling her everything she knew about her long-lost relative. Every time Sister Veronica tried to talk to her about it, a cagey look crossed the nun's face and she changed the subject. Yes, she definitely knew more than she was letting on. But why be so guarded about information that would surely help the baby? What secrets could she possibly be hiding? That was an area that definitely needed some more investigation.

Much as she loved Hope, Sister Veronica knew the nuns needed to help find her a forever home. It just wasn't practical having her in the convent, and for heaven's sake, the baby needed a loving family to help her flourish and grow. And the only person who could answer all the questions surrounding her abandonment, that would eventually help Hope somehow end up in such an environment, was her mother. Drawing herself up to her full height of five feet two-and-a-half inches, and internally steeling herself for any response she might receive, Sister Veronica pressed the doorbell, and rapped four times on the door. Then she stood back, and waited.

2

Rivers of tears gushed silently down Mona Adkins' cheeks as the door slammed in her face. Immediately in darkness, she heard a key turn in the lock, and two bolts sliding into place. The tight gag across her mouth made screaming impossible, and anyway, she suspected such an act would bring immediate punishment from her captor.

As her eyes adjusted to the gloom she looked around, grateful for the dull sliver of daylight oozing under the door. She was sitting in a small cupboard. Locks of lank auburn hair straggled over her shoulders, blood from her recent beating sticking the ends together. Her hands – bound tightly behind her – now pressed down hard on rough wooden floorboards. An old-style boiler rumbled next to her, and she tilted herself the other way, wanting to move as far as possible from the incessant clamour. But being sandwiched between the boiler padding and the cupboard wall meant there was not much space to lean. The dry, stale smell was unpleasant. The rope round her skinny ankles bit into her skin, she couldn't shift her legs without causing them to burn with pain. Craning her head back, she saw a wooden shelf above her. She was boxed in.

Trapped. The tears gushing down her cheeks felt as hot as her airless prison.

Of course she couldn't escape her past. How stupid of her to think she could. But she'd been so close; it had taken years to finally get away from her hometown and the people who'd caused the problems, who made her feel repulsed if a memory of them so much as entered her brain. Well, most of them anyway. For a long while she'd felt hopeful, and it had been an intoxicating feeling. Okay, so working as a prostitute wasn't everyone's dream job and it *certainly* wasn't hers, but it was infinitely better than the situation she'd come from. And it was helping to get her back on her feet. She'd even managed to save some money; she wanted the best for her baby girl. She was planning on giving her a very different childhood to the one she'd had. Baby Asha deserved the world, she was so beautiful and innocent, so unspoilt by the dark forces of the universe. There would just be pure love between them, with absolutely no coercion, control or abuse. She would keep saving, maybe get a new job, and they'd get their own place together, somewhere with good schools and green places to explore.

Pain ripped through Mona's insides as thoughts of her baby flooded her mind. She could practically smell her, that delicious, powdery infant scent. Being away from her made her head ache, her heart hurt and her stomach nauseous. Who knew motherly love could be so powerful? But where was baby Asha now? Was she safe, somewhere in London? *He* better be looking after her. Mona ground her teeth. He better make sure she comes to no harm. She'd left Asha with him for one day, ONE DAY for fuck's sake, and look what happened. But it wasn't his fault she'd been captured, it was hers, she'd been stupid, she should have seen it coming. *He's a good man*, she reassured herself. *But he's weak. He needs to make the right decisions now; the baby's safety depends on it.* Would he suspect what had happened to her? And if he did, would he do something to help her? Then a new thought hit her hard. Shit. He was in danger himself, of course he was. He'd probably be the next to go.

Letting out a guttural groan, with helpless rage suddenly displacing fear, Mona lifted her feet up, then slammed them down hard, smashing her head back intentionally against the cupboard wall. She could feel the rope burn away patches of skin around her ankles and her head ached, but she did it again, then again. She deserved the pain, she needed the pain, it made her feel alive and real. THUMP. CRASH. Was she being foolish? Yes. Did she care? No. Why had she walked into this trap so easily? After all her hard work. For God's sake, why had she not learnt her lesson by now?

Fast, loud footsteps belted up the stairs. The bolts were slid back. The key turned in the lock and the door opened with a bang. Her captor towered above her, waving a studded belt in her face.

'Mona? You're being a bit too noisy, darling. Let's see if we can quiet you down a bit, shall we?' The words were spat out, loud and furious. 'You know I told you to stay quiet. But I should have remembered; you were never any good at following rules, were you?'

The belt came whipping towards her face. In a flash Mona saw that it didn't contain studs, it was riddled with nails...

3

'Yeah?' The thin, pale girl sighed. She couldn't be a day over twenty, Sister Veronica thought, as her heart throbbed with compassion for the sorry-looking creature in front of her. With dark bags under her eyes, unmistakeable needle marks in her arms and a threadbare dressing gown covering her emaciated frame, the girl was the picture of downtrodden exhaustion. At least she wasn't hostile though. Just disinterested with a strangely dead look in her eyes. Sister Veronica had the sudden urge to scoop her up, take her back to the convent and give her a hearty meal. But didn't it say in Galations that we all have to bear our own load, or something to that effect? Perhaps it was best not to interfere. Hopefully the universe had greater intentions for the poor child at some point in the not-too-distant future. Not that she put much stock in that sort of thing anymore. Sister Veronica tutted under her breath as she fought off recent memories of being crushingly disillusioned by the criminal actions of some clergy.

'I'm so sorry to disturb you, my dear, but I was wondering if you could help me. I'm looking for a young lady named Crystal?'

Sister Veronica smiled. 'I'm hoping she might be able to help me find a missing person.'

The young lady stared at her.

'Yeah?' she said. 'I'm Crystal. Who's missing?'

'Ah, that is fantastic news, very pleased to meet you. I'm Sister Veronica from the Convent of the Christian Heart. I'm trying to trace the mother of this baby.' She smiled at the girl as she patted the hood of the pram. 'The baby's mother's not in any trouble or anything, we just need to know she's healthy and safe.' Sister Veronica fumbled in her pocket, retrieving a folded photocopy of Mona's face, then thrust it towards the girl. 'If you wouldn't mind taking a look. Is there any chance you might know her?'

The girl turned her hollow eyes towards the picture and stared for a few seconds.

'Yeah, I know her. That's Mona.'

'Yes. You're absolutely right, she's Mona Adkins. DNA testing has confirmed she's the mother of this little baby, who was left on our convent steps a little while ago. We desperately need to make contact with her, for her and the baby's sake. The police–'

The girl immediately withdrew inside the building at the mere mention of the word. She glanced up and down the road, with fear in her eyes. *Stupid woman*, Sister Veronica reprimanded herself. *Don't scare her off, show her you are both on the same side.*

'Er, the police haven't actually been very helpful,' she went on, changing tack fast. 'So at the convent we've launched our own little investigation into finding Mona. Nothing to do with the police at all. They haven't told us anything so we're not telling them anything.' She leant forward conspiratorially. 'I bet we'll find her before they do, with the fantastic help we've been getting from Mona's friends.'

The girl's bony shoulders relaxed a bit. She hesitated.

'Mona's all right. She's helped me out a bit since I started working round here. Nice girl.' Her voice was flat. 'Different from most of them. Haven't seen her for about a month though. I went to see the baby just after she was born. Cute kid.'

Sister Veronica smiled.

'Ah yes, she is absolutely gorgeous. Although as you can see she prefers sleeping during the day rather than at night.' Sister Veronica rolled her eyes in mock despair. 'She'll have all of us at the convent run ragged with tiredness in no time, I expect.'

The girl shrugged. Her glassy stare drooped down towards the pram.

'Mona's other friends have also told me they haven't seen her for a while,' Sister Veronica went on. 'I've been asking around for a few days now. One of them said she kept herself to herself after the baby was born. That she didn't work much after that. Does that sound familiar?'

'Yeah,' the girl said. 'She started living with that bloke, didn't she?'

Sister Veronica nodded eagerly. So the girl did know something about Mona. This was sounding hopeful.

'Yes,' she said. 'Someone mentioned a man. Did you, er, know him too?'

'Nah.' The girl sighed. 'Never met him. He wasn't there when I went to see the baby. Just heard. You know how talk goes around.'

'That I do. You should hear what some of the Sisters discuss at dinner time in the convent. So much prattling I have to close my eyes sometimes. Er, could you possibly give me Mona's address? No one else has been able to remember it so far.' *Or was willing to break the code of honour among working ladies of the night*, she thought. *They protect each other, and that's very good. But it's not helping me much in this quest.*

The girl met Sister Veronica's gaze for a moment.

'I reckon you're all right,' she said, a few seconds later, nodding her head slightly. 'Mona lives in the top flat over the pub in Dolly Street. But if no one's seen her for a while she's probably moved on. Girls move in and out around here all the time.'

'Thank you so *very* much.' Sister Veronica beamed. 'You really have been a huge help. And I do wish you the very best for your future. If you ever need any help do come and call for me at the convent.'

The girl shot her an odd look, then turned, closing the door behind her.

'Right then, Hope,' Sister Veronica said briskly to the still slumbering child as she swung the pram round. 'Next stop, Dolly Street.'

It didn't take long to find. Sister Veronica said a silent prayer to the universe for having equipped her with local knowledge; one thing about living in the heart of Soho for so many years meant she was easily able to navigate around, and she was thankful for that, it made life much more convenient. She brought the pram to a halt next to the Sailor's Inn, the only pub in Dolly Street, and stared up at the façade of the old Victorian three-storey building. *So Mona lives in the top apartment*, she mused, looking for the front door and finding it to the right of the pub's front.

The top apartment was certainly a rather shabby affair when contrasted with the one below it, whose windows were adorned with well-maintained window boxes. Mona's flat sported a row of dirty windows flanked by frames of peeling paint, and one of the panes was cracked from side to side. *What a mixed bag of people we are in London*, Sister Veronica thought as she studied the two doorbells next to the powder-blue door, wondering which one to press. All so very different, and all living side by side.

As she decided whether to press Flat A or Flat B's bell, the door swung open and a tall, blond-haired man paused on his way out, his young face registering surprise as he came face to face with the old lady on his doorstep.

'Well, hello! Can I help you?' he said, shifting a sports bag on to his shoulder.

'Yes, I rather think you might be able to.' Sister Veronica smiled, stepping back. 'I'm looking for this girl, and was told she might live here?'

The man inspected the photo of Mona hastily thrust towards him. His face clouded over.

'Yes, that's Mona. She lives in the top flat. We're in the middle one.' He gestured towards the window boxes.

Sister Veronica nodded.

'I'm Sister Veronica, I live in the Convent of the Christian Heart in Soho Square,' she said as she folded the photo up again. 'We're trying to trace Mona, as she's the mother of this little baby here, who was left on the convent doorsteps not long ago.'

The man's handsome, tanned face turned a shade paler and his mouth fell open.

'She left her baby with you?' He bent down and looked into the pram. 'I can't believe it, I really can't. Mona had poor taste in men but she loved that baby. I never thought she'd give her up.' He shook his head. 'I really am gobsmacked to hear that.'

Sister Veronica made sympathetic noises and inclined her head slightly, watching with interest as a second, shorter – completely bald – man appeared at the doorway.

'Sorry, I couldn't help overhearing.' The newcomer raised his eyebrows as he rested a hand on the tall man's back. 'No wonder it's been so quiet round here. We haven't heard any crying for at least three weeks, have we, Joel? We were just saying that the other day, weren't we?'

'Yes,' the tall man – Joel – said, turning to him. 'Honestly, I can't believe Mona would dump her baby on a doorstep, can you? She was totally in love with her. She'd actually started to look happy – for once in her life – after she had her, didn't she?'

'So she didn't seem happy before that?' Sister Veronica asked.

'God no,' the shorter man said, resting his other hand on his hip. 'Well, I don't think you could be happy living the life Mona did. She was on the game, and had endless bad relationships. The amount of times we've had to call the police when there was a row going on upstairs.' He shook his head. 'It's been quite quiet since Lance came to live with her, and to be fair the baby didn't make too much noise. Just every now and again. But recently we've actually been able to sleep through the night for once, haven't we?' The two men smiled at each other.

'Lance? Is that her new boyfriend?' Sister Veronica said. 'Is he the father of her baby? There's no father's name registered on the birth certificate, you see, so I was just wondering...'

'Who knows with Mona,' Joel said with a sigh. 'She keeps herself to herself, but from what I can see everything's always so complicated in her life. We've had bailiffs round asking after her, police breaking into her flat, angry men banging on the door, honestly you couldn't make it up. It's a bit of a nightmare to be honest. She's a lost soul, so fragile, like she'd break if you touched her. Not just physically, emotionally too. God knows how she does the job she does, she must be tougher than she looks.'

'The thing is,' Sister Veronica said slowly, thinking hard, 'we're not at all sure it was Mona who left the baby at the convent. She seems to have gone missing, none of the girls round here have seen her for weeks. The police are looking for her too.' She watched them, gauging their reaction.

'Really?' the shorter man breathed. 'Oh my God. That must

be why they broke in to her apartment last week. They were up there for ages, all we could hear was furniture being moved around, like they were looking for something. No one was in there. I just presumed Lance must be a dealer. Sorry, Sister, but you get a lot of them round here, and Mona's been out with a few before.'

'Oh I know what goes on round here, don't worry.' Sister Veronica grimaced. 'Not much surprises me anymore.'

'Yeah, we were convinced that Lance was dealing, weren't we, Gavin?' Joel turned to his partner, a thoughtful expression crossing his face. 'Especially after that night when the strange man showed up and shouted up at their windows for ages.'

'Oh?' Sister Veronica's ears pricked up. 'What was the man saying?'

'It was the weirdest thing,' Joel said, shifting position. 'It was about seven in the evening – I remember that because I'd just finished my shift at the Sailor's and I was desperate for a shower–'

'He comes back smelling like a brewery most nights.' The smaller man winked. 'If I didn't know better I'd think he was up to something.'

'And I couldn't get to the front door because a man was blocking the way,' Joel went on. 'First I thought it was Lance, and that he must have got locked out. From the back it looked like him, the guy had the same chin, long golden hair, although it looked like it could do with a good wash. But when he started shouting, I knew it wasn't.'

'Why? What was the man saying?'

'He just kept shouting, "Lance, I know you're in there. Come and face me like a man". When he turned round to look at me he had tears in his eyes,' Joel said. 'It was really odd.'

'We just thought it was an emotional drug user.' Gavin smiled. 'You get all sorts round here.'

'I was trying to get past him to get my key in the front door,' Joel said. 'I was tired and I just wanted to get home. Gavin was out that evening, weren't you?' He turned to his partner, who nodded. 'So he was no use, I couldn't call him to come down. The guy tried to get inside the front door with me as I pushed it open, and I got a bad feeling from him, so instead, I pushed him back and slammed the door, and went back to the pub. There was something not right about him, I didn't want him in the building.' He frowned.

'Not right?' Sister Veronica repeated.

'No. His eyes looked kind of unhinged. Staring. I just thought he was high, or coming down off something,' Joel said. 'As I was walking to the pub door, he shouted up, "You've broken the promise, Lance. I trusted you. Why did you do it?" Then he started sobbing. I just thought it was more of the melodrama that surrounds Mona, so I had a few drinks in the Sailor's and waited for Gavin to come home.'

'This is interesting,' Sister Veronica said. 'Have you seen Lance or Mona since then?'

'No,' Gavin replied. 'It's been bliss. We just thought they'd left in the night to avoid whoever was looking for Lance. But I had no idea the baby was with you. That's kind of sad, it makes me worry for Mona. We thought she and Lance might settle down, you know? Find some sort of peace together.'

'I don't know how to thank you,' Sister Veronica said, turning the pram. 'You've both been so very helpful. Really. You've given me so much useful information.'

'Just one more thing, Sister,' Joel called, as she made to walk off. 'I didn't talk to Mona much, didn't get much of a chance. But one thing I do remember her saying was that it was so much nicer in Soho than in Somerset. Maybe that's where she grew up? I remember being a bit shocked, as Soho is adorable but I've always thought Somerset is gorgeous.'

'Thank you so much.' Sister Veronica banked the information away, her head spinning. 'I won't take up any more of your time. Have a lovely day, both of you.'

Right, she said to herself as she wheeled the pram away, gurgling noises from under the hood heralding the end of Hope's nap. *Sister Catherine is going to have to tell me everything she knows about Mona, and I'm not accepting any more of her ridiculous evasiveness. Somerset seems a good place to start the conversation.*

4

Art Pendragon drummed his fingers against the pub table, wondering why his son thought it was okay to be late to their meeting. Obedience was the first thing he'd taught his children, and Gareth was usually good at it. Not like the other one, who had chosen the path to hell. He frowned as he thought about Lance, the black sheep of the family. After their mother, Shirley, had left the group – he'd obviously forbidden her from taking his sons with her, telling her to never contact them again – he'd trained the boys so well, told them exactly who they should be, how they should behave, and what they should think. It was a very necessary part of being a leader, and Art knew he was the best one around. The only one, in fact, the Almighty's voice on earth, the messiah, King Arthur. He had triumphantly returned from the Otherworld to save his people in Britain; a fact that had been revealed to him by God in visions and dreams since he was sixteen. Returned to Avalon, the old Glastonbury, where he'd been looked after before he'd died all those centuries ago. Before then he'd believed what his parents had told him; that he was plain old Colin Sacks from Croydon.

Since his first coming, Britain had been invaded in ways Joe

Public was blind to; politicians and their spin-doctoring had taken over people's thought processes. The media had brainwashed everyone into banal stupidity. Different religions – other than the true one: Christianity – that purported to have all the answers, were fuelled by greed, power and authority. The isle had been invaded by people of every culture who were ruining traditional British ways. And that was just for starters. He didn't need to pull a sword out of any stone to know he was the true messiah; anyone with an ounce of sense knew that the sword story was a metaphor for justice for Christianity. Whoever had said the pen was mightier than the sword had been right. And he was proving a leader in this; he – King Arthur – was now mature, and had a clear vision for the future of Britain.

Arthur – Art's – sons were blessed to have been born at the New Avalon Commune; his followers – the New Knights – understood his offspring were spiritual gifts, sent to help spread his word, and he'd made sure the boys digested this as they grew up. Lancelot, the elder of the two, was supposed to take over the role of leader from him when the time came. He'd been primed for it for years. But no, that evil bitch Mona had to go and put doubts in his mind, telling him all sorts of lies and making him deluded and fearful. She'd set him on the path that led straight to hell. Oh, how history really does repeat itself. When he'd first been King Arthur, all those years ago, his son – Lancelot – had fallen out with him over a woman; Guinevere. And now, the fact that Lance had left New Avalon was Mona's doing. He would never forgive her for that. *Never.* Art clenched his fists until the knuckles were white.

'Sorry, Dad.' Gareth's flushed face appeared at the table. He was out of breath, his eyes fearful. 'I couldn't find a parking place. I know I'm a bit late, it won't happen again.'

Art gazed into his son's eyes for a long time, saying nothing. His face, still handsome in its sixty-third year, motionless. *You're correct, Gareth*, the gaze said. *This won't happen again. If I say we're meeting at three o'clock, then we're meeting at three o'clock, not a second afterwards. If this happens again there will be consequences. Is that understood?* Gareth, who had been raised to be exquisitely attuned to his father's thought processes, let his gaze drop. So much knowledge passed silently between them, but only the most alert observer would have grasped a hint of the meaning behind it. This was Art's favourite way of communicating; it was quiet, intimidating, and oh so powerful. When he saw the deferent reaction in his son it reassured him that Gareth was still his. Art had always known it was much better if he did Gareth's thinking for him. In fact, he did everyone's thinking for them. This was why the New Avalon Commune was the harmonious place of integrity that it was; Art steered from the helm, and everyone else learnt the true ways. He was extraordinary, he'd been chosen by God to lead, and he was damn well going to do it and not let anyone stop him from his mission.

Founding New Avalon just outside Glastonbury, Somerset, in 1983 had been the best decision of his life. Slowly, people had joined from all over the country, news of the peaceful commune spreading by word of mouth. By 1997 the number of followers had reached sixty-two, all of them swearing allegiance to the returned messiah, King Arthur, with many babies being born to group members. Shirley had been a delight to start with but had started wanting to be treated equally, or some such feminist rubbish. How could a man and a woman be treated the same? Or more to the point, how could King Arthur be equal to one of his followers? It just didn't make sense. He'd been glad when she'd left, it hadn't been hard deflecting her attempts to contact the boys and after a few years she'd given up.

It had been such a joy to raise his sons and all the other innocents in the right way from the start, away from devilish societal ways of capitalism, greed, immorality and duplicity.

He'd taught them well, he knew he had. But in every rose bush there is a thorn, and in his case her name was Mona. So different from her younger sister Celeste – the beautiful girl who still loved him dearly. Chalk and cheese, those two. Good and bad, innocent and corrupt. One thing was certain; Mona the betrayer had made a grave mistake by going against his will – God's will, and Art was still suffering from her actions today. The ramifications of her accusations had been huge, had nearly destroyed him, with the sullying of his reputation and group followers leaving the commune. It had nearly broken him. But not quite. No, Mona would never have the power to do that. And now he was gaining energy again; God was spiritually feeding him – his favourite King; Arthur – and soon he would be strong enough to do what he needed to do to repair the damage and see justice.

'Sorry,' Gareth muttered again, pushing his hair behind his ears and slowly sitting down opposite his father. Art regarded him. Gareth's features were softer than his, less defined. He watched the light go out of his son's eyes. Good. He'd learn to be more vigilant in future.

Art purposefully said nothing. He would not openly forgive Gareth too soon, that would only cause problems and encourage equilibrium between King and knight. And anyway, they had another transgression to discuss. Gareth must work hard for his father's mercy, earn it. It was the only way he would learn. Art tucked his long, greying, well-conditioned hair behind his ears and waited. Gareth fidgeted in front of him, his dark eyes flickering from his father's stare to the tabletop, then back again. The pub waitress arrived to take an order for Gareth's drink, but Art waved her away. He took a sip of his Guinness and licked his lips.

'Gareth,' he said at last, allowing his brow to furrow. 'I'm worried about you. For so long I was sure you were on the path to salvation. You've been the best pupil, the most attentive, quick to understand the ways of God, and an obedient and loving son to me. But recently, well...' Art let his words trail off, and he gave a small shrug. 'I fear your brother leaving New Avalon has influenced you somewhat. I would hate to see you also turn towards the Devil. Is that a new bag?' He squinted at the black satchel on Gareth's knee. 'My, my, how advertising affects you these days. Have you forgotten, Gareth, that constantly buying new possessions blocks us from God's true will? We become beholden to "stuff" instead of to The Almighty. And that makes him very angry, but it makes Lucifer clap his hands and focus his red eyes on us, does it not?'

'I know – no, no this isn't new,' Gareth stammered. 'Well, I mean it is, but it was free. It came with the laptop. You told me to buy one, Dad. To set up the new website with.'

Art felt a small surge of anger swill across his insides. The boy was right, he had told him to purchase a laptop, told him the exact model to get. But being contradicted was hard to take. Art knew he was very good at controlling his anger these days, in fact he was good at most things. So he smiled.

'Of course, you're quite right. I did. But let's leave discussion of the website to another time. Today I want you to tell me why you've been contacting Lance. Did I give you permission to do this?' Art gained much pleasure from the look of horror that consumed his son's face.

'N-n-no, you didn't give me permission to do that, Dad,' he said. 'But–'

'*But* you did it anyway,' Art said slowly, deliberately. 'And now you're going to tell me why.'

Gareth swallowed.

'I don't really know why. I just... miss him, I suppose. I wanted to know why he left me.'

Art stared at him, wondering how it was possible for Gareth to still be so innocent.

'Oh Gareth, still so ignorant, and after everything I've taught you,' he said, careful not to show any pleasure on his face. The stress in his son's eyes was causing him deep satisfaction. 'Lance didn't leave *you*, he left God. He chose darkness instead of light, hell instead of heaven. He left New Avalon, but more importantly he left me. He knows I'm God's messenger, his voice in the physical world. He knows that to gain eternal life when he passes he must follow my word alone. But the evil temptress Mona turned his mind. She's wicked, and he's weak. I didn't think he would be, but he is. There's no room for weakness, Gareth. Can't you see how that as cracks appeared in Lance's faith in me the Devil crept in to him? He doesn't love you or me, or any of us anymore. Can you see how easy it is for that to happen, for someone who turns away from me to go to the darkness?'

'Yes, Dad.' Gareth nodded. His eyes had tears in them. He'd been looking forward to meeting his dad, had a few website ideas to discuss with him; he'd been so proud to have been put in charge of launching the commune's new webpage. It had been a huge moment in his life because it meant his dad trusted him, was giving him some responsibility. Had made him feel as though Art was taking notice of him for once. But now he realised he'd done wrong, insulted King Arthur who he was so blessed to have as a father, and thrown his salvation into jeopardy. It was only right that his actions should be corrected. He needed to atone for his wrongdoing. But Lance leaving had ripped his heart out. He still loved his brother, even though he understood that this was wrong and self-centred. He'd just wanted to see him, to understand why Lance had left.

'I'm so sorry, I was being selfish, just thinking of my own needs and not the good of New Avalon. It won't happen again.'

Under the table, Gareth rolled up his sleeve and scratched at a scab on his arm. He needed to feel the pain, he deserved the pain. He picked part of the scab off and threw it on the floor. Then he scratched and scratched at the wound until he felt moisture ooze from it.

Art narrowed his eyes, satisfied. Oh yes, Gareth was still his all right, he could see how much agony disappointing his father had caused him. Lance leaving had caused Art pain too, of course. Lance had always been the golden child, the stronger, better-looking boy, so confident and clever. Gareth was more anxious, his face so serious. He was always on the outside of conversations looking in, never at the centre of things. But he was all Art had left now, and he was still loyal and respectful, which was very important.

'Gareth,' Art addressed his son. 'I have great hope that there is still a good chance you will be saved. Just follow my words and you will be well.'

'Yes, Dad,' Gareth said. His sad eyes stared into his father's, while his nails – hidden from view – continued to scratch away at his arm.

'Very good. Listen carefully.' Art leaned forward. 'God has given me this mission, Gareth. He's chosen me to be his voice on earth, He puts words and thoughts in my head, and tells me to share them with you and the other New Knights. I'm asking you to join in the fight against the evils in Britain, help me rid her of this consumerism, capitalism, media obsession and worship of false idols. Do something that matters, Gareth. Something big. Make a stand, make me proud of you.'

5

Mona's stomach contracted and she let out a soft moan, trying to change position and ward off the pain. It had been over twenty-four hours since her captor had last chucked the dry bread through the door. Her hands, now untied, grasped for the water bottle under her knees and she sucked the final drops of liquid out. There was not nearly enough left to quench her deep thirst. Her body was numb, every part of her was so weak. Her joints – forced to bend in unnatural ways for too long in a cramped airing cupboard – were seizing up.

'Asha,' she whispered. 'I love you, baby girl.' She wondered if the universe could transport her words to her baby's heart. Maybe if a feeling for someone was super strong it would transcend time and space. The only thing that mattered was that Asha was safe, well and happy. And very, very loved.

When would the footsteps next ascend the stairs? And when they did would they bring food, drink or punishment? She'd been too weak to make any noise for the last two days. Life was now about survival at the most basic level. Existing. Enduring.

Mona shut her eyes and drifted into a semi-conscious state.

Reality was more comforting like this, blurred and distant. She could let go of everything and just float. And her prison guard couldn't hurt her when she was like this. No one could. She let herself drift further and further away, inviting oblivion to totally engulf her.

6

As dinner at the convent drew to a close, Sister Veronica reflected that it had become a chaotic event since Hope had come to live with them. Perhaps the baby had not napped enough today, but she'd been in a decidedly hostile mood all evening; spurting puree from her mouth at every opportunity, whilst crashing cut-up pieces of fruit and vegetables from her baby tray on to the floor with her fist. The highlight of the meal for Sister Veronica had been when Sister Irene had stood up with a piously depressed expression – as well as orange puree – on her face and exclaimed:

'I cannot live under these conditions for much longer,' before exiting the dining room. No doubt off to write another letter to social services, Sister Veronica had thought, narrowing her eyes at the retreating nun's back.

Or perhaps, Sister Veronica mused, as she wrangled the fretting baby out of the highchair whilst making soothing noises, *Hope just misses her mother. She's bound too, really, it's only natural, and from what the two men were saying it sounds like Mona – with all her faults – really loves her child. Which makes it all the more worrying that the baby's here and Mona is goodness knows where. Oh, how I do wish the police would keep us informed of what they know, it would help soothe my mind to know even the tiniest bit of information. Oh well, I'll just have to pursue the case myself until she's found.*

Sister Veronica hitched the baby on to her hip and turned, to find Sister Catherine snoozing in the chair at the end of the table, her head lolling to one side.

'Catherine. Catherine!' she called, walking over and shaking her friend's shoulder. 'I'm afraid it's time to wake up, I need to talk to you as a matter of urgency.'

The nun rubbed her eyes.

'Did I drop off again? Honestly, that baby will be the end of me.' She yawned.

'I'll tell you what,' Sister Veronica said, knowing she'd probably regret her bargaining strategy later that night, 'If you come to the library now for a chat, I'll look after Hope tonight. How does that sound?'

'All right,' Sister Catherine said groggily, heaving herself up. 'You've got yourself a deal.'

Minutes later the two of them were ensconced in the chilly library, blankets tucked round their knees. Sister Veronica had passed Hope to Mother Superior as she left the kitchen, and the head nun had immediately swept the fretting infant away to chapel, saying it was never too early to learn the benefits of prayer and devotion.

'Right,' Sister Veronica said, looking her friend straight in the eyes. 'I think there's something we need to discuss, isn't there?'

'Is there?' Sister Catherine's cheeks went a shade pinker. Her hands twisted over one another in her lap. 'What's that then?'

Sister Veronica sighed, smoothing out the rug on her knees with her hands.

'Hope's mother, Mona,' she said quietly. 'Although I'm pretty certain you already know that, Catherine.'

The nun opposite her lowered her gaze, exhaling. She sat silently for a minute.

'Right,' she said, as she looked up. 'Yes, sorry, Veronica. I know I've been a bit unhelpful about Mona, but it's not an easy subject for me to talk about, really. You'll understand why in a minute.'

'No problem at all, just take your time,' Sister Veronica said gently. 'But we do need to find Hope's mother, for everyone's sake, Catherine. And please know that I'll treat everything you tell me with the strictest confidentiality.'

Sister Catherine nodded, taking a deep breath.

'Well, as you know, I came over to England from Australia about a year and a half ago,' she said. 'My family are originally from England, Somerset to be precise, but my father emigrated in 1970. The government was offering a ten pound scheme to the British, as Australia wanted help populating its shores, and my father took advantage of it as he thought he'd have a better life there. And he did; he got a good job, built his own house, met my mother, and had us kids. But I still have quite a few relatives in the UK. I know some better than others.'

Sister Veronica's ears pricked up. Sister Catherine's family were originally from Somerset too? And the nice men had said Mona had referenced the same place. She might be getting somewhere at last.

'I did know of Mona before the police told me about her.' A guilty look fixed itself on Sister Catherine's face. 'But, oh Veronica, the shame of it all. I could hardly bear to think of it, let alone tell anyone about it.' She looked down at her hands.

'Tell anyone about what, Catherine?' Sister Veronica asked. 'I hold no judgement for anyone. You can safely tell me absolutely anything.'

'Um...' Sister Catherine struggled to find the words. 'Mona's family are not the kind of people you would want to know. They are some kind of relatives on my father's side, but I've never really found much out about them, to be honest.'

Sister Veronica said nothing, privately thinking she usually rather liked the people no one else wanted to get to know. She'd always been bloody-minded; angry when people became marginalised or oppressed and sad when they suffered.

'They, well, they chose a bad path in life, that's all I know.'

Sister Veronica smiled.

'Come now. I feel there's still a bit more you need to share with me?'

Sister Catherine groaned.

'Fine. I've never met them, but I only know what other relatives have told me. It's just the girls from that family left now, Mona and Celeste. Their father disappeared out of the picture very early on, as far as I know, and their mother passed away several years ago. Mona and Celeste grew up in what you might call a cult.'

Sister Veronica sat up.

'I see,' she said. 'Do you know what it was called?'

'No idea, but they lived in a commune somewhere in Somerset, near Glastonbury, I think. It's very sad really, they were totally brainwashed by all accounts. I heard Mona left the cult under a cloud quite recently, but I had no idea she'd come to sell her body just round the corner from the convent. Poor girl. Oh, the shame of it, Veronica. You must think I'm quite heartless because I find this whole thing so difficult to talk about. But I do feel for Mona, I really do. It's why I agreed to look after her baby for her. But I just didn't think it would do any good to sully her name and the family's reputation any further by connecting us all to the sordid cult she was involved with. Knowing she's a prostitute is bad enough. To be honest, I was hoping Mona would have turned up by now. I thought she might have just gone off somewhere to clear her head for a few days, maybe needed a rest from looking after the baby, you know? Goodness knows, I'm starting to understand how tiring motherhood is now.'

'You've done the best thing by Mona, Catherine, you're looking after her baby for her,' Sister Veronica soothed, leaning forwards to pat her friend's knee. 'So don't you worry about that. But I don't think Mona has just gone for a rest somewhere. Think of that awful tarot card left with Hope, with the word Destruction on it. Why would Mona have left that with her? No, I have a feeling things may be rather more serious, I'm afraid, which is why I'm so desperate to locate her.'

A tear rolled down Sister Catherine's cheek.

'Yes, you're probably right, Veronica,' she said, wiping it away. 'I can see now that I've been a fool to keep this information to myself. It's just I hate the thought of this cult, it's so disreputable and wrong to brainwash people.'

But isn't that what we do here in the Catholic Church? Sister Veronica mused, choosing to keep her thoughts private. *Tell people what to think and what to believe?*

'Now, you said Mona had a sister?' Sister Veronica drew a clean handkerchief from her pocket and passed it to her friend. 'Do you know anything about her? She might be a good person for me to find, sisters can sometimes be so close.'

Sister Catherine wiped her nose and cleared her throat.

'I don't know much about her,' she said. 'Only that her name is Celeste. I've heard she still lives in Somerset somewhere, possibly in Glastonbury. I really have told you all I know now.'

Sister Veronica stared into the nun's eyes and knew that this time, she was telling the truth.

'Thank you, Catherine, and please don't be worried or ashamed. We are all human, and we all do things we regret; I had a cousin who shot himself in the head after losing at gambling one night. His mother never got over it, and quickly went to an early grave herself. It's pain and fear, you see. Eats people up and makes them do strange things. Right,' she said, slapping her knees and standing up, deftly catching the blanket falling off her knee in one hand. 'I know just the person to call. I have a feeling I may need a tech wizard for the next part of my investigation.'

'Investigation? You really are starting to sound like an amateur sleuth, you know, Veronica.' Sister Catherine gave her friend a watery smile as she folded her blanket. 'By the way, how's the crime writing going these days?'

'I haven't had much time for that recently, more's the pity. Real-life sagas keep presenting themselves to me, and they rather get in the way of the creative process. Now I must dash. There's someone I need to phone before evening prayers.'

As Sister Catherine watched Sister Veronica leave the library, she realised she hadn't seen the old nun so sprightly for weeks. There was a veritable spring in her step now. She smiled. It was good to see the old girl back to her normal self after the whole Jamie Markham debacle. That had been such a worrying time for them all. As she rose to her feet, Sister Catherine wondered who in the world her friend could so urgently need to call at this time of night...

7

As Melissa Carlton popped another piece of gum in her mouth and chewed slowly, she began to have second thoughts. Had jacking in her job at the *Women of the World* magazine been such a good idea? Maybe not, she mused, staring out of her study window at the gridlocked South West London traffic, but at least it had given her the opportunity to be a truly free agent, to spread her journalistic wings. The only problem was, she was desperate for a good story to cover, and nothing was currently grabbing her. The present political situation was tedious, and anyway, every other bloody journo in the country was writing about it. Human interest stories usually got her attention, but there didn't seem to be anything new on offer to get her teeth into.

Not like last month's writing bonanza, she thought, blowing a bubble that immediately burst onto a long strand of her pink-and-blonde hair. Fuck, she'd have to cut it out; no point even trying to get gum out of tangles, she knew that from experience. As she rummaged for the sharp scissors, memories of her recent time travelling around in secret with Sister Veronica flooded her head; the night-time trip to France, the illicit and terrible events at the Vatican, meeting her new and wonderful partner Chris, formally Bishop Hammett, who was now away in Rome trying to sort out his laicisation from the Catholic Church. Blimey, she missed him like crazy and it was making her grumpy.

It had certainly been a whirlwind adventure with Sister Veronica and one that had netted her four high-profile articles in different magazines and newspapers. And it had prompted her resignation from her steady job at *Women of the World*; she'd suddenly seen what she could achieve with a bit of travel and bloody-minded investigative effort. But now... things had kind of dried up, and it was worrying her. The rent wouldn't pay itself and she'd had to buy cheaper food for the cat, who had been highly offended by this and was now ignoring her.

The bleeping from her mobile phone cut through her reverie.

'Hello?' Why did her voice always sound so moody when she answered the phone?

'Ah, Melissa. Are you free to speak?'

'Sister!' Melissa instantly felt a thousand times better. 'This is so strange, I was just thinking about you. How's the arm?'

'Much better, my dear. Just a little stiffness left now but they cut the plaster off last week, thank the Saints. It was such a nuisance lugging it about. Listen, I have something to ask you, although I know you're probably terribly busy.'

'Not as busy as I'd like to be.' Melissa grimaced. 'Work's a bit slow at the moment.'

'Excellent, then the universe may be bringing us together once more,' Sister Veronica said. 'I have a new problem that I'm dealing with, and would cherish any help you could give me. Do you remember the little baby I told you about who was abandoned on the convent steps?'

Melissa confirmed that she did.

'Well she's still here, and we are still trying to trace her mother. The police aren't telling us anything, of course, and I'm not sure it's a priority for them, what with all the other troubles we have around here; so much drug dealing, and that's just the start of it. So I've been doing a bit of digging myself, and some lovely locals have pointed me in the direction of Glastonbury in Somerset. It might be where the baby's aunt lives, and I need to find her address, but that would involve searching on the computer, and you know how inept I am at that sort of thing. I know this business might not appeal to you, it's all tarot cards, prostitutes and a disappearance, but if you could spare the time–'

'Oh Sister, this is right up my street.' Melissa sat up, a smile creeping across her face. 'I can't tell you how bored I've been this week. Just tell me where to meet you and I'll be there with bells on.'

'Excellent,' Sister Veronica said. 'And thank you so much, my dear. I can't wait to see you. Now I must tell you that when we do find her address I'm planning on tracking her down, which may involve a trip to the West Country. If you don't have anything better to do you could always accompany me? It might help the search for Mona if you could write a little story about it? Maybe interview her sister if we find her? I know you're terribly clever at that sort of thing.'

'It would be my pleasure.' Melissa punched the air with her free hand. Yes! Blimey, Sister Veronica was a crafty old goat. She'd clearly had the whole idea planned before she'd even called her. 'Shall I meet you at the convent tomorrow morning?'

'Ah, no,' Sister Veronica said quickly. 'It's probably best if Mother Superior doesn't see you actually, Melissa. There's a slight problem there with her keeping a close eye on me after the whole Jamie Markham affair. I don't want to worry her with this, so I'm trying to be as discreet as possible; she'd only stay up all night performing a novena for my soul if she knew how involved I was, and that sort of carry on exhausts her for days. Perhaps I could meet you at the library in Soho around ten tomorrow morning?'

'Perfect.' Melissa grinned. 'I can't wait to see you again, Sister.'

They said their goodbyes and Melissa put down the phone. She grabbed a bag and stuffed her laptop into it, suddenly eager to get everything ready for the next day's adventure. Good God, that woman was a sly old fox; so sharp she'd cut herself one day. And a good friend now, too. They'd been through a lot together already and it looked like their adventures weren't over just yet. Slapping a new nicotine patch on to the inside of her arm and sweeping her hair up into a messy bun, Melissa caught sight of herself in the mirror. She hadn't looked this happy for days. My, my, how one little phone call could unexpectedly change the direction of life.

8

Lucan Butler exhaled, his heart heavy, as he watched King Arthur speaking to his crowd of followers from the centre of the room. As usual, they'd met in the Great Hall, a large canvased structure in the heart of the New Avalon compound, with huge ornate red dragons painted along its interior walls. The words '*Rex Quondam, Rexque Futurus*' were emblazoned above the door. Everyone present knew their meaning: '*King once, and king in the future*'. In homage to the age-old round table tradition, they always gathered in a large circular formation, and Art took centre stage on a small podium, so that he could see everyone's faces, whichever direction he chose to face while talking.

There were only twenty-four New Knights left now and six of them were children. So many people had left after Mona had spoken out, revealing truths to them about Art's depravities that had sent shock waves through the commune. Of course, many people who stayed had utterly refuted Mona's claims, denouncing her even more viciously than Art did. Lucan had stayed because he had nowhere else to go; at fifty-two years old he'd spent the best part of his life at New Avalon, and considered his friends there to be his family. Just the thought of leaving caused his heart to hurt. But the doubts he had about Art kept on growing, and each time he listened to the king talk he felt empty and soulless. And he felt guilty for this, because deep down he still wondered if Art *was* the chosen one. And he was terrified of going to hell, as Art repeatedly told all his followers that they indisputably would if they were ever disloyal to him. All Lucan knew was that what had started out as a place of love and safety had morphed – over the years – into the exact opposite. He couldn't talk freely about his feelings to most other followers, of course, because to do so would be heretical, and there were now spies in every corner.

Since Mona left, suspicion abounded in New Avalon, and many people were becoming paranoid. Art encouraged his followers to tell on each other if signs of disloyalty to him became apparent; Lucan would never forget seeing his good friend Kay hauled into the centre of a meeting to be publicly condemned by Art. She'd also become disillusioned by the king's increasingly bizarre ways and demands, but was much more courageous and vocal in her questioning of this than him. Her punishment was being humiliated by Art in front of the whole group, stripped of her privileges, and told she was ruined and on the path to hell. She now lived in isolation in the furthest hut from the Great Hall, and was forbidden from joining in with commune life until Art was satisfied she'd repented, which he showed no sign of, flatly refusing to talk about her and becoming angry if anyone dared mention her name. Lucan still visited Kay, of course, brought her secret food parcels whenever he could, as her daily rationing was abysmal. She'd lost so much weight since the night of her banishment, and her hair was now falling out in clumps, which Lucan suspected was to do with stress. She wanted to leave New Avalon, but like all the New Knights, had given Art all her money and possessions on arrival, and had been out of regular society for so long that she feared she wouldn't be able to survive if she went back.

Lucan – not his real name, but one given to him on his arrival at New Avalon – knew he was a coward for living the way he did; inwardly disgusted with Art, but outwardly conforming to New Avalon's rules and ways of life. But what else could he do? He shook out his long mane of hair. The sense of desperation within him seemed stronger every day. All males and females at the group were encouraged to grow their hair long and keep it parted in the centre because, as Art reiterated from time to time, this was how he – as the first King Arthur – wore his all those years ago. Lucan's gaze transferred from Art to the figure moving to his right. Ah, Celeste, the beauty of the group and Art's right-hand woman. As loyal to New Avalon as her sister Mona had been rebellious.

As usual, Celeste's golden hair was worn long, and she was dressed in her red Renaissance gown, one of her favourites, that Lucan knew was inspired more by modern paintings of the old King Arthur's wife Guinevere than any historically accurate attire. He bit his lip, hating the fakery at New Avalon. All the men and boys had to wear tunics and all the women had to wear skirts or dresses, but as there wasn't much information on what King Arthur and Guinevere actually wore all those centuries ago, the New Knights made up their own styles based on more modern depictions of King Arthur. And this seemed kind of inauthentic to Lucan. He would have preferred it if they'd been allowed to wear normal clothes. If the New Knights went 'outside' – their term for the world beyond the commune's walls, the girls were allowed to wear trousers if whatever task they were undertaking required it. But not inside. Art, of course, was the only one who wore a robe. But Lucan didn't think the original King Arthur would have worn a robe all the time. Certainly not when he was fighting, it would have got in the way.

He'd come to think of New Avalon as shallow, which pained him, as his first ten years there had been the happiest of his life.

In 1990, at the age of twenty-two, Lucan – then called Simon – had left Bristol University with an accounting degree, and a deep desire to never become an accountant. The Conservatives were in power, and John Major had just taken over from Margaret Thatcher's reign of capitalism. Lucan's young socialist tendencies were causing him to increasingly distrust mainstream society, much to his parents' vexation, and during a particularly enlightening night at Glastonbury Festival he'd met New Knights Bors and Geraint by the stone circle, becoming captivated with their praise of Art and New Avalon, and the law-abiding, loving commune they described living in. Within a month, he'd moved from London to Somerset, and found all of Bors and Geraint's claims to be true. Art – oozing with charisma – had welcomed him with open arms, and Lucan had immediately felt like he belonged at the commune, feeling accepted and loved in ways he'd never experienced before. It had been such a relief to find fellow human beings who also rejected the worst parts of capitalism, and who wanted to live a different kind of life, full of loyalty to one's friends, fairness and justice. It was fun to paint the placards and banners that were arrayed around the exterior of the compound fence, with socialist slogans like Trotsky's 'Cleanse evil, oppression and violence' and Malcolm X's 'You show me a capitalist and I'll show you a bloodsucker'. Their leader, he discovered, was not above calling on more modern theorists to drum home his message.

There were some battered old communal cars at the site that anyone with a driving licence was welcome to use. A shared kitchen, where the New Knights took it in turns to cook for each other. Everyone chipped in with care for the children, playing games with them, teaching them how to read, write and draw. They were all home-schooled, of course, Art loved the fact that these 'innocents' – as he called them – were having a life totally immersed in his philosophies from the very start. This kind of shared living was heart-warming, Lucan found, well certainly at the beginning of his time there. It felt like it was the way humans were meant to exist, all together, helping one another. Feeling looked after and valued was wonderful for a while. But then things had started to change.

Too much of a deep thinker to ever fully accept that Art was in fact the returned messiah King Arthur, Lucan had ignored his doubts about that little detail in favour of belonging to a group. He needed New Avalon, it really was his own idea of utopia come true and he yearned to be fully immersed in it and accepted by everyone. So if that meant agreeing that Art was the returned king, it was a concession he would willingly make. And anyway, King Arthur was supposed to return when the nation needed a saviour, and Lucan found that idea beguiling; especially as he felt Britain did indeed need to be saved from itself. And what the hell did it matter if Art said he was King Arthur? In a way, it was kind of endearing, a bit like role-play for adults. That's what he'd thought to start with, anyway.

When he'd first arrived, Art was everything he wanted in a father figure; strong, chivalrous, handsome, charming, someone who put a strong emphasis on loyalty, honour and morality. A big contrast with his biological father who in 1990 had just been made redundant and spent his days drinking and watching darts on the television, only getting up to shuffle to the fridge to get himself another beer. His mother hadn't been much better, always whinging about something, always depressed. It hadn't been hard to separate from his parents – or the Externals, as outsiders were known – as Art required all new recruits to do.

That little detail about Art actually being the returned messiah had come to occupy the centre of his existence over the years, and he now couldn't remember how to have full confidence in his own thoughts. This worried him. But he'd been told so often that he must follow Art's ways, or risk falling into ruin and going to hell, that he now felt confused, believing that in some way Art must be correct. Or was he? Lucan really didn't know. On the one hand it was an absurd idea to think you were actually a returned mythical character, and on the other it seemed completely plausible, now that he knew Art. But Art and the New Knights never seemed to achieve anything with their ideals, with all the battling against capitalism that Art lectured them about. It was all talk and hardly any action, a few posters and protests, but nothing big. He'd begun to feel that Art's interest didn't actually lie in changing the world, but in having power and control over the group. Once, a long while ago, Lucan would have gone to Art for help with his thoughts, explained that he was having a bit of trouble. But he couldn't now, no way. He no longer trusted him, and that was disturbing to admit.

'Why are you whispering?' Art's sharp tones cut through his daydream. The comments were directed towards two of the young children, Savannah and Star, stationed to the side of their mothers. 'God doesn't like whispering.' He bent down to speak directly into their faces. 'Only serpents whisper with their flickering tongues. Come and see me afterwards and I will hand out penalties to you. You must learn, girls, that no one else talks when I am speaking.'

He watched Celeste smile up at Art, pride all over her face, and wondered, not for the first time, how she could sleep with that old man. Granted, he looked younger than he was, but still, there was near enough forty years age difference between them. Followers at New Avalon were encouraged to be free with their sexuality, because, as Art always said, true freedom meant emancipation in all areas. Celeste and Art had been in a relationship for three years now, although they often shared their beds with others, of course, as was the way there. Lucan reckoned Celeste must have slept with most of the men at the compound, she certainly gave off that impression. But not with him though. Oh no. His heart belonged to her sister.

A stabbing pain caused Lucan to lean forwards as he remembered Mona; he'd really loved that girl. *Really* loved her. Their encounters had been infrequent, usually after one of the mead-soaked great dinners the New Knights shared a few times a year. Yes, he'd been thirty years her senior, but it hadn't seemed to matter for Mona, who was a breath of fresh air, and an amazing conversationalist, much more intelligent than Celeste in his opinion. Her departure had left him reeling, he hadn't seen it coming, everything had happened so suddenly. Her revelations, the awful truth. The rejection had broken him. And what she'd revealed about Art that terrible night before she'd gone had cut him to the core. Lucan exhaled, trying to steady his emotions. In his heart he knew he would do anything to help Mona, keep her safe from the evils of this world; now as prevalent in New Avalon as they were anywhere. He'd told no one about his recent, secret trip to London. Art had just thought he was out on a stock run for the Glastonbury Café he worked in. That hadn't caused any problems, as the king liked his followers to bring in as much revenue as possible. Lucan hugged his knowledge to himself as his mind ticked fast. He now knew what his next move would be. He was going to save Mona's soul. He hated what she'd become, but he was strong enough to help her, he knew he was.

9

'Hello, Melissa,' Sister Veronica barked. She glared at the gurgling baby lying in the pram next to her chair. She'd been cursing her bargaining tool with Sister Catherine all morning; what a ridiculous idea to say she'd look after the baby all night. Goodness gracious, what a kerfuffle it had been; there'd been wriggling, playing, crying, winding, a tiny bit of sleeping, then more crying and playing. She'd barely made it down to breakfast on time, Sister Agnes had already started on the washing-up when she and Hope had eventually sat down, and all that remained on the table were some cold slices of toast.

She was sitting at the central table in Soho's community library, the pram at her side, surrounded by shelving units containing rows of higgledy-piggledy books. Far from being Sister Veronica's ideal place of book worship – she was indeed one to revere books – it was more like a supermarket, always noisy, with too many people, the wares on offer presented with less flare than duty by the tired-looking librarians.

'Ooooh, this must be the new addition to the convent,' Melissa cooed, bending down to stroke Hope's cheek. She was too used to her friend's changeable moods to take any notice of her abrasive tone. 'She's absolutely adorable.'

'She's an adorable insomniac,' Sister Veronica said. 'Slept in two-hour blocks last night, at four thirty-seven this morning we were both up and pacing round my room, weren't we, Hope?' Another glare.

'Hope?' Melissa said. 'Is that her name? It's pretty.'

After explaining how the baby's temporary name came about, and accepting Melissa's offer of going for a strong coffee and perhaps some custard cream biscuits after their library chat, Sister Veronica got down to business.

'So what we need to do,' she said, watching Melissa open her laptop, 'is find the address of Mona Adkins' sister, Celeste. Sister Catherine believes she may still be living in a cult in Glastonbury.'

'A cult, ooh now that is interesting,' Melissa breathed, tapping in her password. 'I've always found the idea of cults fascinating, haven't you? Wondered what makes people join them, and give up their lives with their friends and families?'

'No,' Sister Veronica said shortly. 'Nothing is more dangerous than stopping people thinking for themselves.' *Although the parallels between this claim and some practices of my own religion are very uncomfortable and need deeper investigation*, she added to herself. Although many would disagree.

'Right, let's have a look.' Melissa leaned forward, scanning the results of her Google search. 'Look, Sister. We've got a result already. I put in "Celeste Adkins Glastonbury" into the search engine and it says "Celeste's Cards: A Tarot Reading service". The address is Goddess World on Glastonbury High Street.'

Sister Veronica rocketed forward and stared at the screen.

'Tarot cards?' she said.

'Yes, look.'

Sister Veronica stared at the words in front of her. This was too much of a connection to be a mere coincidence, surely? Melissa clicked on the link and they watched as a page full of bewitching designs loaded against a purple background.

'"Celeste is an experienced tarot card reader",' Melissa read. '"She offers individual, couple and group readings. A clairsentient psychic, Celeste gives positive readings that provide clarity and hope to her clients, enabling them to forge deeper connections with their intuition and energies. With her guidance, clients find it possible to heal and remove obstacles in their lives, while delving deeper into an understanding of their true nature".'

'She's very pretty,' Sister Veronica said, staring at the blonde-haired beauty at the centre of the screen. 'And she promises the earth. If only life were that simple. Do you think she looks like Mona at all?'

They spent a few minutes studying Mona's photo and comparing it to the face on the screen. The images had been taken at two such different times in the girls' lives, their inner energy seemed the biggest contrast between the two; Celeste looked glowing whereas Mona looked run-down.

'Maybe a bit,' Melissa said. 'Their noses are similar, and so are their mouths. It's hard to tell, it's not a great picture of Mona.'

'I know,' Sister Veronica agreed. 'It was the best I could get from her Soho working friends. Does it mention this Celeste's surname anywhere? Adkins?'

Melissa studied the page.

'Not that I can see,' she said. 'But there's the tarot card connection, and that's a great starting point. I remember you telling me about the card left with Hope. But it's hard to imagine that this girl would be involved, she looks so lovely.'

'Never be fooled by external appearances, Melissa,' Sister Veronica said, reaching out to rock the pram back and forth as Hope was becoming increasingly vocal. 'Many crimes have been committed by beautiful people, you know. I mean look at that monster Ted Bundy, from the United States. He killed at least thirty young women, but because he was good-looking and seemed respectable, everybody liked him and didn't want to believe he'd committed the murders. I read an article about him once at the doctors while I was waiting for Sister Agnes to get her new arthritis medicine prescribed. Even the judge at his trial congratulated him for being a nice person. People can be so blind sometimes, and so very stupid.'

They spent a few minutes scrolling through the rest of the search results. Then at Sister Veronica's request Melissa spent some time looking up cults in and around Glastonbury, with the nun marvelling at her dexterous use of the keyboard. Sister Veronica was very suspicious of digital technology in general and was still refusing to get a phone, despite Melissa's assurances that it would make her life a lot easier. The new style of phones, with all the mysterious swiping of the screens, looked far too complicated, and anyway she enjoyed going incognito whenever she felt like it, and couldn't think of anything worse than people being able to contact her whenever they wanted. Sister Irene would no doubt be constantly ringing with complaints and Mother Superior would be able to keep continuous tabs on her. No thank you, that sort of thing was definitely not for her. Now a pad of paper and a pen, that was where true happiness lay. Her latest crime novel – started many months ago and still not finished, more's the pity – would be penned entirely on paper, exactly as it should be. Stationery shops were her favourite type of place to browse around; all that paper – stacked and tidily bound together – was exciting, the untapped potential in it seemed to hum whenever she perused the shelves looking for yet another new, bigger, better notepad. Laptops and computers just didn't do that. The only hum they omitted was due to the ridiculous amount of electricity flowing through them, and frankly she could do without that sort of carry on.

'There are no other obvious leads here, Sister,' Melissa said after a while. 'Celeste sounds like the best starting point we've got. And by the way, cults aren't exactly going to label themselves as "a cult" on the internet, they probably don't even think of themselves like that, so we'd never have any luck finding it that way. So does this mean we're going on a field trip to Glastonbury to have our tarot cards read?'

'Yes, I believe that's exactly what we should do,' Sister Veronica said, thinking, still rocking the pram, with Hope amusing herself by making loud squawking noises. 'Although how I'm going to get this past Mother Superior I do not know. She's watching me like a hawk these days. It's a blasted pain, to tell you the truth.'

Melissa snorted with laughter.

'You're such a rebel, Sister,' she said. 'You shouldn't be a nun, you should be a revolutionary.'

'One can be both, you know, my dear,' Sister Veronica said, a smile playing at the corners of her mouth. 'Although I'm nowhere near extraordinary enough to be a revolutionary. I'm just a stubborn old woman who can't keep her nose out of trouble.'

'Aha, I have an idea,' Melissa said, her eyes suddenly glinting. 'Glastonbury's an amazing place, jam-packed with every kind of spiritual teaching you could think of. I love it there, I stayed in a hippy bed and breakfast on the high street with a friend a few years ago. There are so many different courses on offer, like circle training, mystical earth tours, cartomancy and obviously tarot. There are also retreats. Why don't you explain to Mother Superior that you're still a bit shaken after everything that went on while you were trying to find Jamie's killer, and that you would benefit from going on a retreat for a few days. Surely she can't object to that, isn't that what nuns do?'

'Yes, nuns do go on retreats, Melissa.' Sister Veronica broke into a hearty laugh. 'But not usually in places of alternative spirituality. Nevertheless, you have given me an idea. Leave it with me, and I'll see what I can do.'

'Hang on, my phone's ringing.' Melissa fumbled in her handbag, retrieving it. 'Chris!' she said loudly into the handset, standing up. 'How are you, babe? Oh my God, I miss you so much, it's unreal.'

'Shhh,' Sister Veronica hissed. 'Melissa! Good Lord above, we *are* in a library, and you are being *very* loud.'

An old man with a white moustache and beard – ensconced on a corner sofa – flicked his newspaper down and stared at Melissa, undisguised irritation on his face. Noisy and busy though the library was, their party seemed to have exceeded even the place's usual standards of unrest.

'Right,' Sister Veronica said firmly, standing up and folding the laptop, before putting it back in Melissa's bag. 'I think it's time we left, Hope, don't you? We seem to be making quite a scene.'

Hope gave a happy scream in reply and thrashed her arms and legs around.

'What do you mean you have to stay in Rome for another two weeks?' Melissa's voice was getting even louder. 'Babe! I thought you were coming back next Tuesday? I'm really missing you. Why is this taking so long to sort out?'

Sister Veronica shepherded Melissa out of the library door and towards the nearest café, using the pram as a guiding shield. Despite the incessant noise around her, a plan was forming in her tired mind, and she hoped it was one Mother Superior would accept. But the wily head of the convent was no fool. Yes, she was dramatic, that was for sure; the amount of histrionics the nuns endured from her was unfathomable, and Sister Veronica privately thought she should be on the stage, cast as a tragic Shakespearean heroine. But underneath all the spectacle the woman was intelligent, you could see it in her eyes. Getting her to agree to another trip away so soon after Sister Veronica's last impromptu disappearance from Soho Square may be difficult, she reflected, if not impossible. But this was important and she needed to find a way to make it work...

10

Lancelot Pendragon closed his eyes. He was sinking into the sofa. The ketamine – taking a strong hold of him now – was both shutting his brain down while opening it up in a different dimension. He'd been up, now he needed to come down, it made scientific sense. He could hear chatting, although he was pretty sure no one in the room was talking. It had been a heavy night at The Orb club and it was getting more intense right now.

He'd arrived at The Orb, one of his usual haunts, by himself. Met some regulars in the chill-out zone, and they'd shared their fares amongst themselves whilst sweaty ravers piled into the room around them. He couldn't remember all the drugs he'd taken in the club but he was pretty sure cocaine, ecstasy and base speed were in the mix. He'd danced to the banging trance music for what seemed like hours, and in the end he'd successfully reached the level of zoned-out intensity that he always tried to attain. He, Lance Pendragon, had become one with the music and the universe. At that moment, it was all that mattered. It meant he didn't have to think about anything else, none of the appalling circumstances in his life that he might have to face without drugs.

Mona – no. He didn't want to think about bloody Mona again. Why had that name popped into his head? She was nothing but trouble. She didn't even know if the baby was his. Slag. His father – God, why was his brain tormenting him with these people, this pain? Lance forced his eyes open and leaned forwards, shaking his hair from his eyes. Three other people, two men and one woman, were lying on the floor, miles away in their private worlds of drug-induced delirium. He didn't know them, had just accepted an invitation from the girl he'd chatted to in the club to go back to her flat. Quite standard, he did this sort of thing all the time.

His pile of white powdery ketamine was on the side table, amid Rizla papers, bongs, and glasses of water. Bending forwards, ignoring the pain in his chest and the way he couldn't quite catch his breath, and guiding his trembling hand towards his Oyster card, Lance cut two more fat lines and snorted them. Then he lay back, his eyelids drooping. The prickling in his skinny arms and legs didn't matter now. His numb lips were interesting. If memories of Mona and his father thought they could torment him, they were wrong. Lance was in control, and nothing would get the better of him. No one would EVER dominate and manipulate him, not one more time. His father would NEVER again cause the deep depression Lance had waded through for so many years, internally battling with the ideology he was taught and the actuality of living with his autocratic, insane parent. Medication was a wonderful thing. He'd given up on having any sort of relationship with his mother, Shirley, years ago. When he'd finally found out her address and contacted her, aged nineteen, she'd made it quite clear she couldn't see him anymore, that he belonged to Art, not her. All the more reason to bump up his self-medication, it eased the pain of rejection. And, of course, he knew where Mona was, but he wasn't going to tell that to the fucking pigs who'd been sniffing around his friends, asking questions. Mona didn't matter now. No one mattered now. He was a free agent at last, a lone wolf. A smile broke out across his face as he sank willingly into oblivion. He rather hoped he'd die this time.

11

'Sister Veronica, what on earth is wrong with you?' Mother Superior, Sister Julia Augusta, said, lowering her half-rim reading glasses. She leant forward and stared. The nuns were gathered in the chilly convent library, each partaking of an activity of their choice. Hope, asleep for once, slumbered quietly in her baby bouncer near the fireplace, a pink knitted blanket tucked around her cosily. Mother Superior *had* been trying to read the next page of *The Awakening of Miss Prim: A Novel*, but the soft moaning coming from Sister Veronica's hard-backed chair was putting her off. 'Are you ill?'

'I don't think she's poorly, Mother, not in a physical sense anyway,' Sister Agnes said in hushed tones. Sister Veronica had taken her best friend at the convent into her confidence after returning from her meeting with Melissa, explaining the necessity of her travels to Glastonbury and the opposition this suggestion was likely to meet from Sister Julia. Agnes had, of course, agreed to help her, smiling gleefully at the thought of giving their dramatic head nun a taste of her own medicine for once. 'I think she's suffering mentally.'

At this point Sister Veronica took the opportunity of

slumping sideways with a low groan. Her head came to rest on the cool wall, and she shifted her knees until her book fell to the floor.

'I see.' Mother Superior narrowed her eyes. 'How strange. She looked perfectly well at afternoon tea, indeed I believe she ate the majority of the chocolate biscuits, much to Sister Irene's sorrow. I wonder what could have happened to her over the last couple of hours to cause the sorry state I see before me?'

'Mother Superior!' Sister Agnes said. 'How can you be so heartless? You know very well that Sister Veronica has endured the most horrific times recently. And she has borne her suffering quietly and heroically to the point where I think we have all become blind to what she's going through.'

Agnes' words, although hammed up for the purpose of Sister Julia, nevertheless touched a raw nerve inside Sister Veronica, and the undealt with pain and shock of the evils she'd stumbled upon during her quest to right the wrongs done to children of the ordained overtook her. Weeks of pent-up stress bubbled to the surface and before she knew it huge sobs were shaking her body, rivers of tears flowing down her cheeks.

'Veronica.' Sister Agnes – her face registering genuine shock – hurried over to her friend, grasping her hand tightly. 'Oh, I'm so sorry. There, there, my dear, you have a good cry. It will make you feel much better.'

Mother Superior watched, aghast, as Sister Pemii, Sister Catherine and their new novice nun, Sister Anne crowded round the prone Sister Veronica, stroking her hands and knees and making soothing noises. Sister Irene, sitting at a desk in the corner, put her copy of *The Devil's Advocate* down, regarding the proceedings with a steely gaze.

'Well, I–' Sister Julia said. This was most unusual, she'd never seen Sister Veronica in a state of such undoing. 'I didn't mean to be harsh, Veronica, and I'm sorry if it seemed that way.

Of course you have been through many trials recently. You just seemed to be coping so well. Perhaps it was a mistake for you to come back to the convent so soon.'

'Oh yes, she returned too quickly.' Sister Agnes turned, tears in her own eyes now. It was unbearable to watch her friend in real pain, she'd had no idea her words would be so upsetting. But she had promised to help her friend reach her desired goal. 'I think she needs a break, somewhere peaceful.'

'Perhaps the convent in the Scottish Highlands would be an ideal place?' Sister Irene's reedy voice said. 'There's nothing more relaxing than the sight of lochs, I always say. Good for the soul. No one else around to trouble you.'

Sister Agnes glared at her.

'I think we should ask Sister Veronica where she'd like to go, don't you, Irene?' Sister Agnes said, her tone sharp. 'After all, if she is going to go away to recuperate it needs to be a place she feels comfortable with.'

'Somerset,' Sister Veronica mumbled through her tears. 'I've always loved it there. So green and peaceful. I feel it calling me.'

Sister Irene rolled her eyes.

'Yes, yes, Somerset it is.' Mother Superior flapped her hands, as though wanting the whole scene in front of her to go away. 'Great Saints in Heaven above, I've never seen such a carry on. And in the convent library too.' She put a hand to her forehead. 'I feel quite weak myself now. I'm going to chapel, I need sustenance. Agnes, you can help Veronica now, can't you?'

'Yes, of course,' Sister Agnes said to Sister Julia's departing back. She bent down, wrinkles creasing her forehead.

'I think you really do need a break, Veronica,' she whispered, as her friend's noisy sobs diminished. 'Honestly, you had me quite worried there for a minute.'

Sister Veronica shifted herself into an upright position, and the other nuns melted away, taking up their activities once again.

'Sorry.' She sniffed. 'I don't know what came over me, Agnes. All this pain inside me just welled up as you spoke.'

'And that's exactly why you need to get away,' Sister Agnes said. 'Although I'm not sure throwing yourself into another potentially difficult situation is the right way to go. I hate to say it, but perhaps Sister Irene has a point. Maybe you would benefit more from a complete rest, away from the whole Mona-and-baby situation–'

'No.' Sister Veronica sat upright, anger flushing through her cheeks. 'Sorry, Agnes, but I have to do this. Can't you see? I've been sitting around in this convent for years, being pretty useless, not helping anyone much. But what happened with Jamie showed me how hardly anyone is doing anything about the suffering in this world. If I don't help this baby then who will? The police? Do you really think they are going to put themselves out to get to the bottom of this? If I don't locate Mona and bring this case with Hope to some resolution, I fear social services will dump her with a foster family and that will be that. She'll be forgotten about, or adopted out and she'll never have a chance to know the truth about her parents. I know what that's like, Agnes. Don't forget what happened with my father. Please, you've helped me so much this evening. Now I just need to secure a place close to Glastonbury.' She exhaled.

Sister Agnes wound her hands together, her arthritic knuckles red and swollen.

'Oh, Veronica, you are wonderful. And you're making me feel quite guilty. I suppose I'm also rather useless, sitting in this convent, not able to do much other than pray these days.'

'No, Agnes,' Sister Veronica said. 'You help in your own way, everybody does really. Perhaps I was being too judgemental. I suppose what I mean is, that not many people go the extra mile to help someone. You can't, you have too much physical pain to deal with yourself. But you help people here and in the community, like you did with me just now. And that is rather wonderful. Perhaps I'm just being an old fool, but I passionately feel that I must carry on trying to find Mona. That's all.'

'Then we'll make it happen,' Sister Agnes said, her voice firm, as Sister Veronica rose to her feet. 'Don't you worry, Veronica, we'll have you off to Glastonbury in no time.'

12

Art's face remained expressionless as he watched Lucan talking to Celeste. The New Knights were seated quietly at round tables in the Food Hall, munching warm bread rolls filled with shredded pork. They knew better than to make a din at meals. Art liked to have things quiet and orderly; it was much more civilised, he said. A delicious meaty aroma was filling the canvassed space. Cooking and cleaning were communal activities at New Avalon; everyone was expected to pull their weight, including the children. Some were better at this than others and Art had no problem letting it be known who wasn't working hard enough.

The Food Hall, like the Great Hall – the place of their regular meetings – had snippets of Art's manifesto emblazoned on the walls. *'We are the chosen ones'*, *'We will battle the evils of the world together'*, *'King Arthur, the Messiah, has returned to save his people'*, *'Loyalty, Honour and Integrity are key'*, *'We reject sin and strive for salvation'*, *'We are one family, we need no others'*, *'The New Knights are peaceful warriors'* and *'We will continue to battle dark forces, and save those who come to us for redemption'*.

Something wasn't right. It wasn't the fact that Lucan was

talking to Celeste that was bothering him, after all, sexual freedom was a gift they all shared at New Avalon, and jealousies from one partner to another were quickly ridiculed, usually in public by Art at meetings. Anyway, Art knew Celeste belonged to him. She always had and she always would, no matter who she spent the night with. If he actually thought her heart was leaving his and turning towards another's, well, now that would be a different story. It was the fact that he knew Lucan wasn't telling him something, and that cut to the core of Art's philosophy about absolute loyalty and honour. He must know everything that went on at his commune, or it wouldn't work. Look what had happened with Mona and Lance; they had no doubt been plotting their departure for weeks, maybe months, before it had happened, and he hadn't suspected a thing. But he was vigilant now, and he'd had his eye on Lucan for a while. Knew he visited that damn whore Kay, who Art never wanted to see again, knew he took her food. He was mixing with the wrong company. Once, Lucan had been one of his most trusted knights. But now he couldn't rely on him at all. Art couldn't put his finger on exactly why this was, Lucan was still doing and saying all the right things. But something in his eyes told a different story. Also, God had recently imbued Art with the gift of knowing; an almost psychic ability to tell when someone wasn't being straightforward with him. This meant that God wanted him to deal with people like Lucan, who were showing signs of bringing more trouble to the community. And deal with them he would.

'Celeste, you better get going or you'll be late for your shift at Goddess World.' Art made sure his smile was kind as he wandered slowly over to the chatting couple. She looked up at him, surprise registering on her face. 'I'm only telling you because I care. I know you wouldn't want to keep your clients waiting.' Art stroked her hair.

Lucan grinned up at Art.

'Hey, Big King,' he said, using his usual affectionate address for his leader. 'Do you want me to look over the accounts later? I know I haven't done that for a while, but I've been busy with more shifts at the café.'

'Yes, Lucan, that would be good.' Art turned his gaze on to him, as Celeste gathered up her flowing skirt and stood to give Art a kiss on the cheek. 'Our income is very prosperous at the moment I believe, much helped by you, of course. As you know, I always value your expert opinion on the books.'

'Right, I'll be off then, boys.' Celeste picked up her jewelled handbag. Her lips parted, forming the beautiful smile that captured so many hearts at New Avalon. 'I have many fortunes to tell and lives to heal. I'll be seeing you later.' She turned and headed for the door.

Her eyes, bright as usual, looked particularly sensual today, Art thought. He suspected he was in for another wonderful night. He waited until she had left the Food Hall, then sat down next to Lucan.

'Is there anything you want to tell me, brother?' he said, staring Lucan straight in the eyes. 'Anything at all?'

'What? No.' Lucan laughed. 'I'm afraid you know all the news that I do, Big King. It's one of the downfalls of living together in a commune.'

'One of the downfalls.' Art rolled the words around in his mouth slowly. 'Tell me, what are the other downfalls of living here? Come now, be honest.'

Lucan laughed, but Art saw the change in his eyes. They were playing a game now, and both of them knew it. But Art was damned if he'd let another man get the better of him.

'Oh you know.' Lucan's tone was light. 'I don't always get my favourite spot here in the Food Hall. And sometimes all the bigger portions are gone. Oh yes, and little Tristan in the hut next to mine enjoys waking me up at the crack of dawn; he loves an early morning loud rampage.' All the adults at the commune had their own huts, Art found that it made partner-sharing so much more accessible.

Art chuckled, but his eyes were hard.

'Is that so?' he said. 'Only little downfalls then, eh?' He sat and stared at Lucan, who stared back. Art always found silence to be a powerful tool. It unnerved people.

'How's Kay getting on?' Art said, several minutes later. He enjoyed seeing Lucan start with surprise. Kay's name hadn't left Art's lips for weeks, his followers knew she was usually an absolute no-go topic for him.

'She's, er, fine, Art,' Lucan said slowly. 'I know she'd love to start joining in with things again soon, if you think it's time.'

Art exhaled.

'Tell me, brother,' he said. 'What are the three main tenets we live our lives by here?'

'Integrity, loyalty and honour,' Lucan said.

'And did Kay show me she could follow these beliefs?' Art said.

'No. Well, yes and no,' Lucan said. 'She honestly didn't mean to offend you, Art. It's just that–'

'Brother. Anyone who talks behind my back, criticises our life here and complains and whines is not only offending me, they are offending God,' Art said. 'Who am I to go against God's will? He has given me the power to look into people's souls, and what I saw in Kay is nothing but rot and ruin. To have her back among us would only jeopardise our own salvation. Rot grows if left untended. The only thing we can all do is pray for her and ask the Lord to redeem her blackened heart.'

Lucan nodded.

'You're right, Art,' he said. 'I can see that now.'

Art stared at him.

'I can see into your soul, too, Lucan,' he said. 'And do you know what I find there?'

'What?' The first glimmer of apprehension flickered across Lucan's eyes.

'Ah, now that's for me to know, and you to find out.' Art smiled, standing up. 'Rest assured, Lucan, I mean to rid New Avalon of any other decay and corruption that I find. There's no place for sinners in paradise. Morgana is helping me with this. Now there's a lady with a pure, honest soul; I'm quite sure she would die for me if I asked her to.' Art took a moment to enjoy this reverie, the ultimate show of loyalty a person could commit for him. 'You'd be surprised if you knew all the titbits of information Morgana's been feeding me with recently. Oh yes, you'd be very surprised.' He watched Lucan's eyes flit over to the majestic middle-aged woman on a nearby table. 'We shall be discussing many of them at the next meeting. But of course, you have nothing to worry about, do you, brother? As you clearly want me to believe your soul and mind are as clean as they once were when I first allowed you to live here. For your own sake, I hope they are.' With that, Art walked over to the buxom Morgana, who as usual was spilling out of her bodice, her dyed-black, shoulder-length hair pulled into a half ponytail – a style he privately thought was too young for her. He bent down to whisper something in her ear.

Lucan sat and stared straight ahead for several minutes after Art had left him. Surely Art couldn't know what he'd done? He'd been so careful to cover his tracks, told no one at New Avalon or anywhere else. Perhaps the man *was* psychic? Sorcery had abounded within the Arthurian story for centuries, and Lucan was no longer clear whether he believed in it or not. Stress tightened his chest, but he was careful not to let his external appearance change. What on earth was he going to do now? How much did Art know?

13

Sister Veronica sniffed the air. A veritable feast of incense and food smells assaulted her nose. So this was Glastonbury Town, eh? Was she imagining it, or was there a tangible quality to the energy here, one that was so different to Soho's cosmopolitan urban one? It seemed at once a place that was alive, yet apathetic; the musicians in front of St John the Baptist's Church encapsulated this – two were standing and singing, banging drums as though their life depended on it, but the third lay on the paving stones in front of them, barely managing to tap his tambourine. The shops sold a mixture of conventional and outlandish wares; from baked beans to witches' broomsticks, dog food to love potions. The unassuming buildings of the high street – that sported an assortment of stone and colourful facades – were like a stage set for the mixture of weird and wonderful people that trudged up and down the hill. So far she'd seen men dressed as women, witches, pagans, hippies, very conventional couples that looked like they'd stepped straight out of *Town and Country* magazine (she'd read a copy at the doctor's, most informative), women dressed in white feathery garments and groups of listless teenagers. The biggest shock had been a bald-headed man who'd stopped right in front of them, opened his mouth, and let out a high-pitched shriek.

Sister Catherine, on finding out her friend was booked into a spiritual guest house in Glastonbury, had surrendered to an epiphany.

'Oh *do* take Hope with you,' she'd begged. Sister Veronica, who'd secretly been hoping for this result, stared into Sister Catherine's tired eyes. 'She's much more bonded with you than me, and I'm going to go mad, Sister, MAD, if I don't get some proper sleep soon. Just take her and I'll square it with Mother Superior when you've left, I'll explain that Hope was looking a bit peaky and needed a holiday too.'

Of course, Sister Veronica had agreed, privately knowing that Sister Julia would be incensed with rage when she found out the baby had gone too, but prepared to weather that storm when the time came. Act now and worry later, had always been her motto.

'Do you like it here, Hope? Do you like it?' Melissa cooed in the baby's ear. She'd hardly put her down since their travels had started at London's King's Cross station, dressing her today in an outfit she'd bought – a soft green-and-yellow, long-sleeved stripy dress with matching tights and hat. Sister Veronica privately suspected that it would do Hope good to stretch out in the pram for a bit, but Melissa and the baby seemed so happy she didn't like to suggest it.

'Gah,' Hope said, waving her fist in the air.

'Look, Sister, Hope likes Glastonbury,' Melissa said. 'She's given it the wave of approval.'

'Yes, very good,' Sister Veronica said absent-mindedly. She'd spotted a shopfront that boasted the name Goddess World in swirly writing above its large window. It was sandwiched between Arthur's Pet Supplies and The Witch's Cauldron. 'Look,' she said. 'We're here. You should probably take that infernal gum out of your mouth now, it's rude to chew when you're meeting new people.'

'All right, bossy boots.' Melissa laughed and spat it into a nearby bin. 'It's actually nicotine gum, Sister. I'm trying not to smoke cigarettes any more, which is a healthy life choice. You should be supporting me with that.'

'Yes, yes, quite so,' Sister Veronica mumbled, not listening to a word her friend was saying. Her attention was fully focused on the shop, and what they might find in there.

Ignoring the sudden onset of nerves flitting around in her stomach, she pushed the pram determinedly through the front door, causing a bell to jangle. Melissa and Hope followed close behind.

Racks of unusually beautiful clothes in greens, dark pinks, black and aquamarines were packed together so tightly that at first Sister Veronica felt like she'd walked straight into a wardrobe. Where was the counter? Some hearty shoving with the pram – causing a cascade of dresses and hangers to fall to the ground – soon located it.

An older woman with frizzy red hair sat behind it, filing her nails. She was definitely not who Sister Veronica had been expecting to see. The woman looked up, her lined face wearing a bored expression.

'You all right?'

'Ah yes, quite well, thank you. Actually, we are looking for Celeste Adkins, and were rather hoping to find her here.' Sister Veronica stared down briefly at the array of crystal balls before her. Good grief, did people really buy this kind of stuff?

'Have you got an appointment or are you hoping for a drop-in service?' the woman said.

Sister Veronica turned to Melissa.

'Er, drop-in, please,' Melissa said quickly, hanging up the last of the dresses scattered by Sister Veronica.

The woman stood up and went down a little corridor behind the counter that was lined with piles of messily-stacked boxes.

'Celeste?' the lady shouted. 'Are you free? There's people here hoping for a reading.'

'Just coming,' a voice shouted back.

'She'll be with you in a minute,' the woman said, resuming her place on her stool and picking up her nail file. Sister Veronica stood and stared up at the musical instruments hanging from the ceiling, while Melissa took Hope around the shop, showing her the pretty colours.

Footsteps could be heard springing lightly down some stairs, then a girl who couldn't be more than mid-twenties breezed down the corridor and into the shop. Sister Veronica found herself mesmerised by the girl's face. She had such bright eyes, brown in colour but brimming with unbridled, wild energy. A flowery headband sat on top of her golden hair, and she wore a pale-blue bodice – neatly done up – over a long white skirt.

'Is it a group reading?' Celeste smiled at them, revealing a dazzling set of teeth.

'Er, yes,' Sister Veronica said. 'Sort of.'

'Come this way,' she beckoned, waving them round the side of the counter. 'Probably best to leave the pram with Liz, I don't think it will fit past these boxes. Is that all right, Liz?'

'Suppose so,' Liz grunted.

Sister Veronica followed Celeste up a very narrow flight of wonky stairs, Melissa and Hope at her heels. At the top was a landing, chock full with more boxes, some with clothes bursting over their sides.

'Sorry, it's a bit cramped up here,' Celeste called over her shoulder. 'I promise it will be better once we get into my room.'

She led them through one room that looked like a study, and then into an adjoining room.

'Wow,' Melissa breathed, hitching Hope onto her hip as she walked through the door. 'This is so lovely, Celeste.'

'Thank you.' The young lady smiled. 'I decorated it myself.'

Sister Veronica had never seen anything like it. Swathes of pale voile fabric were hung across the ceiling in waves. Rivers of fairy lights hung down like icicles between the folds and they lit up the room in a magical way, which was otherwise dark due to the golden taffeta curtains draped over the windows.

Magical? Sister Veronica reprimanded herself. *Now don't get carried away for goodness' sake. It's very pretty but we are here for research purposes and you need to keep a clear head.*

Celeste gestured towards the large cushions that lay either side of the low rectangular coffee table in the centre of the room.

'Please, choose a pew. I've got a soft pillow here the baby can lie on.'

Minutes later, Sister Veronica and Melissa were stationed on satin cushions, and Hope was lying happily on her back on a silk pillow, staring up at the lights.

'Now,' Celeste said with a smile. 'Are you related? Mother and daughter, I'm guessing?'

Melissa snorted with laughter.

'Er, no, not related. We're just friends.'

Celeste nodded.

'Of course, my mistake. Now do you have a preference for which card deck I use? I have Psycards, the Angel cards or the Forest of Enchantment with me today.' She pointed towards the different packs, neatly lined up at the end of the table.

'Actually, Celeste,' Sister Veronica said, 'before we get started, there's something we wanted to talk to you about.'

The girl looked up, her eyes wide.

'Talk to me?'

'Yes. Now there's no easy way to introduce this topic, so I'll just come out with it,' Sister Veronica said, biting down the awkwardness of the situation. 'We're looking for someone we believe may be your sister, Mona Adkins.'

An unrecognisable emotion flickered across Celeste's face. She sat up straighter.

'I see,' she said. 'Who are you, please?'

'Of course, how very ill-mannered of me.' Sister Veronica smiled gently. 'I should have introduced myself right at the start. I am Sister Veronica Angelica, I live and work at the Convent of the Christian Heart in London.'

'And I'm Melissa,' Melissa said with a warm smile. 'We're so sorry for this unexpected intrusion, Celeste. It's just that we do need to find Mona. She's the mother of this little baby here, Hope, who was left on the convent steps a few weeks ago.'

Sister Veronica filled Celeste in on a brief rundown of events, including how Sister Catherine – a distant relative of the Adkins girls – had been temporarily granted custody of Hope, how the baby was living with them at the convent while the nuns and police tried to locate her mother, who had seemingly disappeared for the time being. How they had come to Glastonbury after finding Celeste's name on 'this internet', and how they were really hoping she could shed some light on Mona's whereabouts.

'Hope?' Celeste breathed, turning her eyes towards the baby. 'So this beautiful little thing is my niece?'

'Yes, if you're Mona's sibling?' Sister Veronica said.

'Yes, Mona's my sister,' Celeste said, still staring at the baby, her eyes wide. 'But I've never heard of Sister Catherine.'

'Ah, fantastic.' Sister Veronica let out a big breath. Excellent. They had a tangible lead at last. The girl was answering their questions, albeit with short answers. But maybe she would warm up a bit if they kept pressing her. What luck it had been to find her so easily.

'I'm afraid Mona and I haven't spoken for nearly three years,'

Celeste went on. 'We had a falling out, and I haven't seen her since. That's all I can tell you about her, really.'

The optimism rising in Sister Veronica's heart plummeted back down again.

'Right,' she said. 'I'm very sorry to hear that. Do you mind if I ask you some questions, Celeste?'

'Ask away, although I'm not sure how helpful I'll be,' Celeste said. She was still staring at the baby, absolutely entranced by her small relative.

'We heard that you and Mona grew up in a, ah, commune, is that right?'

'Sort of,' Celeste said. 'It's a beautiful place of shared living, just outside Glastonbury Town.'

'And there's no chance Mona would have gone back there?' Sister Veronica said, watching Celeste's face carefully.

'No,' Celeste said. *Aha*, Sister Veronica thought. *There it is, the briefest of emotions in her eyes, what is it – disgust? It must have been a bad falling out.*

'And no one there might know where she could be?'

'Sister,' Celeste at last took her eyes from the baby and stared at the nun opposite her, 'Mona chose to cut ties with all of us when she left. It was sad, but there it is. It was her choice, her business. I had no idea where she'd gone, and I didn't know I was an auntie to this gorgeous bundle here until you told me just now. Like I said, I wish I could be more help, but I really don't know where Mona is, and I'm the last person she'd come to if she was in trouble.'

'If you don't mind,' Melissa said, 'can I ask what your falling out was about?'

Celeste hesitated, her face blank.

'I can't really remember,' she said. 'You know what families are like.'

'And the place you lived in is called...' Melissa said.

'New Avalon.'

'It sounds lovely,' Melissa said with a sigh.

'It is.'

'Do you still live there?'

Another pause.

'Yes,' Celeste said. She sighed. 'Shall we get back to your reading?' The girl's face was no longer full of open friendliness. 'I have another client arriving soon.'

'Yes, of course,' Sister Veronica said. 'Just one last thing, did Mona have any enemies that you know of?'

A hint of a smirk whisked across Celeste's mouth.

'Who, Mona?' she said. 'Of course not. She's such a lovely girl.'

'Thank you,' Sister Veronica said. She shifted position. 'If you have another client coming we can always leave now, and pay you the full price of a normal session? You've been ever so helpful.'

'No, stay a minute, Sister.' Celeste reached across and grabbed the packet of Psycards. 'I'd love to do a reading for you.' She shuffled the cards with the ease of an expert, then in one whoosh of a movement spread them face down across the coffee table. 'Just pick four and hand them to me.'

Sending up a silent prayer to the universe to forgive her if she was, in fact, transgressing any metaphysical rules, Sister Veronica did as she was asked. Celeste arranged the cards in a square, then slowly turned them over.

Two gasps filled the room.

'It's that card again.' Sister Veronica's heart raced into a pounding gallop. 'Destruction. It's the same one that was left on top of Hope.'

'Oh, Sister.' Celeste clapped her hands to her mouth as she stared at the four cards in front of her. 'I hate to tell you this, but you're in danger. You must leave Glastonbury at once, and go back to London.'

'What do you mean?' Melissa said, her tone sharp, leaning forwards.

'First, we have the time in your life in question.' Celeste pointed to the top left card. 'It clearly says: Now. Next, we have your future,' she pointed to the card underneath it, 'prison. This can be an emotional or psychological prison, not just a physical one. Then, we have the likely course of action if you don't heed the cards' warnings.' She pointed to the top right-hand card. 'Destruction. And lastly the outcome.' She pointed to the bottom right card. 'Death.'

'What a load of tosh and nonsense,' Sister Veronica said loudly, heaving herself to her feet. 'I'm certainly not in prison and I have no plans to die, I'm far too busy for that sort of carry on. What I am in need of is a nice cup of tea and perhaps a custard cream. Come on, Melissa, we've taken up enough of Celeste's time.'

'Thank you so much for answering our questions.' Melissa picked up Hope, who was chewing on her fist. 'I think this little lady is hungry too.'

Celeste, her face now ghostly white, rose gracefully to her feet.

'Before you go, would it be all right if I gave my niece a cuddle?' She tried to smile but her face was strained. 'It would mean so much to me.'

'Of course,' Melissa said, handing the baby over. Celeste hugged her close but Hope wriggled uncomfortably in her arms, straining to get back to Melissa.

'Don't take any notice,' Sister Veronica said as she made for the door. 'It's just because she doesn't know you and she gets ever so grumpy when she's hungry. Thank you, Celeste. You've been incredibly helpful. And I apologise again for our rude, unannounced invasion.'

As they left Celeste behind in her room, and made their way out of the shop, blinking as daylight hit them, Melissa whistled.

'Blimey,' she said in a low voice. 'What did you make of all that?'

'On the whole, we now have more questions than answers,' Sister Veronica growled, heading for the nearest café, The Chocolate Berry. 'Although I'll tell you something, I'm never having my tarot cards read again. What a load of codswallop.'

14

Confusion mixed with resignation alerted Lance to his surroundings. Machines and monitors emitting beeping sounds; the humming of ventilators, the long notes exuding from blood pressure contraptions and the high-pitched trilling of infusion devices. He was back in intensive care. Again. For God's sake, how hard was it to accidentally die? He hated himself for not having the courage to actually take his own life with purpose. Just always hoped that a drug-fuelled blackness would handily slide him from life to death without him having to do much. And to think, Art always said he was the brave one. But then his father had got a lot of things wrong.

His eyes flickered open but the brilliant daylight pouring in was too bright. He tried again a few minutes later, and this time took in the cannula inserted into his arm, that had two tubes winding out of it, leading all the way up to bags of fluid suspended above his bed.

The horrible feeling of sobriety was making Lance's brain ache. Because now he had feelings he didn't want and he couldn't block them out. When Mona had left him behind after their row, after sad old Gareth had come shouting up at their window, he'd vowed to spend the rest of his life in as much of a drug-fuelled haze as was possible. He wouldn't be hurting anyone, he wouldn't be in anyone's way. No one needed or wanted him anyway, so he'd doubted whether anyone would even notice. With the remains of the money he'd stolen from his father, Lance had successfully funded his newly chosen hedonistic lifestyle for three weeks, during which time he'd been taken to hospital twice. This time was the third, and appeared – from the feeding tube shoved down his throat – more serious than the last.

'Oh good, you're awake.' A nurse bustled in and placed a small monitor on his finger. 'You're lucky, you know. We nearly lost you.'

If only, Lance thought. *Why didn't you just let me go? What use am I here on earth?*

'The police were here last night,' the nurse said, pulling a clipboard from a shelf at the end of his bed. 'Wanted to talk to you about a missing girl or something. They told me to ring them if you pulled through, but I'll leave it a day or two, until you've got some strength back.'

Missing girl. Mona. The words went round in Lance's head. She wasn't actually missing though, was she? Just didn't want to be found. They'd been silly to think it would work between them, him and Mona. After they'd left New Avalon they'd gone their separate ways for a while, trying to forge new lives and desperate not to be found by Art. Then Lance, weak and broken by too much heavy living, had found Mona a few months ago. Devastated that the silly girl had got into prostitution. She was so much better than that. But her spirit had been wrecked at New Avalon, he understood that now. He should have helped her, supported her more. But instead he just numbed his own emotional wounds with drugs.

Pain stabbed through Lance as he relived the moment Mona

told him she couldn't be sure whether he was Asha's father or not. Now that had hurt. He'd had to soothe that agony with an enormous amount of skunk. He loved that baby girl like she was his own. Maybe she was his. Who else's would she be? Mona wouldn't say, just that a couple of clients' condoms had burst so she could be theirs. But he wasn't fit to be a father, not at the moment. Try as he might, he just couldn't keep making the right choices. The baby deserved more than that. She deserved more than he could give her right now. He couldn't even remember where Asha was. Was she with her mother? Probably, Mona loved that child more than anything. Why wouldn't she be with her mother? Lance couldn't make sense of his thoughts but there was something nagging at the back of his mind, something about baby Asha. Had he left her with a babysitter? He'd been so out of his brain the last day he'd seen her, he could hardly remember anything about it at all. Ah well, she was probably with Mona again now.

A wave of exhaustion swamped him. Yes, he would do the right thing and talk to the police, he decided, as sleep crept through his brain. Mona might not want to be found, but the fact that the police were looking for her made him worry. What if something had happened after all? She'd been so excited to get that invitation. And surprised. She'd told him not to bother looking for her after she'd left, that she didn't need him and his bloody family ruining her life again. 'How did Gareth know my address?' she'd yelled in his face. 'How? He'll tell Art. Just leave me alone,' she'd said. So he had. But now he knew he'd tell the police everything she'd told him about where she was going, about the strange invitation and who it was from. He didn't want anything bad to happen to Mona, not after what she'd been through. And it was the least he could do after she'd taken him in. Yes, he reflected before the veil of sleep finally dropped. It would be the first positive choice he'd made for a while.

15

Sister Veronica sat in The Chocolate Berry's garden next to a statue of a large wicker stag, minding the now slumbering Hope, full and content after a bottle of milk. Waiting for Melissa to appear with the tea and biscuits, she gazed around with the observation of the writer she yearned to be, drinking in the unfamiliar – yet strangely enjoyable – environment. As in Celeste's room, fairy lights abounded, arranged tastefully along the fences and across the Emerald Green shrubs. Wisteria cascaded down and peeping out between its vines were hanging baskets and wrought-iron decorations in the shape of masks and hearts. Broomsticks, propped in the garden corners, received Sister Veronica's most suspicious stares; clearly people round here worshipped relics of witchcraft – or Wicca, as Melissa insisted on calling it. She wasn't a judgemental person, she told herself, but broomsticks and cauldrons were pushing her limits of acceptance just a bit too far. Although, she reflected, many Catholic relics were still worshipped around the world today, and surely only God and the universe can say who's got it right and wrong?

Melissa appeared at the doorway, balancing a tray laden

with goodies, soon weaving her way round the tables where couples and groups laughed and chatted. Minutes later, the welcome taste of tea, and the tang of a pumpkin coffee cake – apparently custard creams weren't on the menu – were soothing her soul.

'Well,' Melissa said a little while later, licking her lips. 'What did you make of Celeste then, Sister?'

'A complex character.' Sister Veronica glanced at the baby, still snoozing – her green-and-yellow hat drifting down over her eyes, before laying her fork down. 'She became more and more guarded as we asked the questions, which perhaps is understandable given that we imposed ourselves unexpectedly, but she certainly wasn't going to give away much, was she?' Melissa shook her head. 'What we know so far from her,' Sister Veronica went on, 'is that she *is* Mona's sister, she claims they had a falling out and haven't spoken for nearly three years and she had no idea she was an aunt to Hope. One of her most interesting revelations was that she still lives in a commune, or cult, called New Avalon – well done for getting that out of her.'

'Yes, I thought we could look that up, now we've got a name for it,' Melissa said, reaching for her bag and pulling out her laptop.

She tapped in her password and soon, the two of them were staring at a webpage on the screen.

'New Avalon looks like a veritable utopia,' Sister Veronica said, taking in the photos of orchards and fields full of smiling children and adults as Melissa scrolled down slowly.

'Yeah, looks like paradise,' Melissa breathed. 'They're all wearing old-fashioned clothes, how sweet. And they've all got long hair. Look at those wooden huts, they look like something pixies or fairies would live in.'

'Hang on, what does it say here?' Sister Veronica rested her hand lightly on Melissa's arm. '"New Avalon is a low impact site two miles from Glastonbury Town, made up from thirty acres of land",' she read. '"The land consists of fields, orchards, woodland and gardens. We own cows and chickens, so can access milk and eggs every day. We also grow our own vegetables; everyone here works together on the land, although several members also hold jobs in Glastonbury and Wells. Residents at New Avalon have taken on the spirit of King Arthur and his knights, in the very best tradition of Somerset history; King Arthur was taken to Glastonbury Tor to heal following his injuries in the Battle of Camlann, and New Avalon pays homage to the return of the messianic king."'

'Interesting,' Melissa said. 'I kind of want to go and live there myself.'

'But have you noticed,' Sister Veronica sat back and folded her arms, 'they are not giving much detail away here. It's all presented in a vague kind of way, the photos only show groups of people some way off, never up close. There is no mention of a leader, or individuals who run the place. It's almost like an image is being presented here to the world, but not much of the actual reality of it. And what's all this about the return of King Arthur?'

'Oh, Sister, you're getting cynical in your old age.' Melissa laughed, reaching for the teapot. 'Haven't you noticed how alternative it is round here? It's a safe place for people to want to express themselves outside mainstream looks and beliefs; the amount of witches, druids, pagans and goddesses I've seen today is unreal. And the myth of King Arthur has always been attached to Glastonbury, hasn't it? They're probably a group of peaceful hippies, living the way they want to, not doing anyone any harm.'

'Hmm.' Sister Veronica's brow furrowed. 'Appearances can be misleading though. Why shut yourself away in a commune to do all this? Why not just live among the townsfolk?'

'But what's wrong with having some privacy and being a bit different from everyone else?' Melissa smiled. 'If I didn't know you better, Sister, I'd think you were being a teeny bit judgemental.'

'I am *not*.' Sister Veronica sat up. 'I rather like it here, actually. But remember we are investigating the disappearance of Mona, Melissa, and to be quite frank Celeste didn't seem at all bothered that her own flesh and blood may have come to some harm. The only loyalty and care she showed was for New Avalon. And Sister Catherine called it a cult.'

'Sister Catherine would probably call the Liberal Democrat party a cult, Sister,' Melissa said. 'Remember, I lived with you guys for a while, and I wouldn't exactly describe any of you as socialists.'

'Well I hope you're right.' Sister Veronica picked up her mug. 'But I think it needs more investigation.'

'Excuse me.' A tall, bearded man – seated with a quiet group of friends at a nearby table – turned his chair round and stared from Sister Veronica to Melissa. 'I couldn't help overhearing. I heard you talking about New Avalon.'

'Yes?' Sister Veronica said. 'Do you know it?'

'Know it? I used to live there,' the man said, a dark cloud passing over his face. 'And if you have any intention of visiting it, I would advise you to forget that idea right away. The place is evil. Best decision of my life to get out of there.'

'Ha,' Sister Veronica said, her eyes glinting. 'Would you be so kind as to join us for a while? I think there are some questions we need to ask you.'

16

Art lit a cigarette and stared at Morgana, anger making his eyes appear darker than normal.

'You fucking what?'

'Lance,' Morgana repeated, tucking her black hair behind her ears, 'is in intensive care in St Francis' Hospital in Peckham.'

Art smashed his fist down on his desk with venom.

'And you know this because?'

'I do a regular call round of the hospitals since Gareth told me he was sure Lance would have got back into drugs. You know what he was like when he was here, got himself in a right mess a few times. I pretended to be his mother. They told me he's in a serious but stable condition.' Morgana regarded Art with motherly concern. He was her everything; she revered his power to lead and control, always had since joining the commune in 1998. She hated how Mona had nearly destroyed him, had spent many nights soothing, cajoling and listening as he ranted about revenge. Deep down Morgana knew she was in love with Art, but she was also intelligent enough to know she wasn't his type; too old, too plump. So she settled for second best, which was to be his confidante. And recently, his spy. She knew she was useful to him, knew her ability to research – she had been a rising academic before deciding to join New Avalon, a piece of ethnographic research into fringe religious groups had resulted in her actually joining one – meant that she was good at finding things out, tracking down information, even the stuff that people wanted to hide. She was a details person, always had been. Wasn't satisfied until she had researched any matter that interested her to the absolute limit of available knowledge.

'What fucking right does that bitch have to destroy my boy?' Morgana noticed Art's hand was shaking as he puffed on his cigarette. 'It's bound to be her doing, it's always Mona's fault when things go wrong. You mark my words, she's been feeding him drugs, making him weak so he will do her bidding. It's her fault that he left, and it's her fault that he's come to harm. I'm going to fucking kill her.'

Morgana sighed. Life had just begun to take on a semblance of normality following Mona's accusations of abuse. It had taken her nearly three years to build Art up, to bolster his spirits and help him regain the belief in the community that he'd once had. And now she could see all that crumbling before her eyes. Art would not recover from this news quickly, and she'd debated whether or not to tell him. But if he ever found out she'd kept this knowledge from him, he would punish her, quite rightly, like he punished all transgressors. Morgana knew she was good at keeping secrets; it had been necessary to become like that at an early age given what went on in her family back in Aberystwyth as she was growing up. The things that had gone on in her home, away from prying eyes, had definitely been at odds with the strict Baptist faith her parents pretended to follow. She'd never told anyone about all of that. But the only person she shared *most* things with was Art.

'Does Gareth know?' Art flicked his cigarette into an ashtray and stood up.

'No, not yet. I've only told you.'

'Good, don't tell him, or anyone else. He'll only go and do something bloody stupid. I can't believe it.' Art picked up a book from the corner of his desk and hurled it across the room. 'My son. Come to this.'

'Calm down,' Morgana soothed. 'There's every chance he'll pull through. He's got your genes, remember, he's a strong fighter.'

But Art wasn't listening. He walked round his desk, bent down, opened a cupboard, and started throwing items onto the floor.

'What are you doing?' Morgana stood up, worry etched on her face. Maybe she shouldn't have told Art after all...

'Looking for my bag. I'm going to London.'

'Oh, Art, do you think that's wise? After everything that happened?' She couldn't bear being away from him for more than a few hours, needed to be near his presence to keep her feeling centred and balanced.

'You don't have children, Morgana, so you won't understand.' Art turned, fury in his eyes. 'Of course I'm going to fucking London. Now get out of my way and stop whining at me.'

Morgana turned and walked out of the study, tears glistening in the corners of her eyes. That had stung.

No, of course Art was right to speak to me like that, she concluded after a few minutes thought as she walked towards her hut. *He's a powerful, passionate person, and I've just given him terrible news. I probably said it in the wrong way, it was my fault. I deserved it. Leaders are always assertive, they have to be. I love him.* But still, the tears flowed down her cheeks.

17

Sister Veronica and Melissa introduced themselves to the man as he pulled his chair up to their table. The noise levels were rising around them as people relaxed, and by the looks of the drinks being brought out by waitresses, The Chocolate Berry café turned into a bar in the evening.

'I'm Carter,' he said. 'Although at New Avalon I was known as Lamorak.'

'Why the two names?' Melissa asked, leaning forward. Their new friend was certainly attractive. If she wasn't so in love with Chris, well... she might be very interested.

'All the men are given new names after they join, when Art knights them during the initiation service. He never seemed so bothered about the women, although some chose new names for themselves. The men's ones are names of the original King Arthur's knights, although at one point, when the commune was very popular, I believe Art ran out of those and had to start being creative. Lamorak was apparently one of King Arthur's more successful knights.'

'Humble brag,' Melissa said, laughing.

'Sorry,' Sister Veronica said, blinking. 'Can I just stop you there. Who is Art? And why is he knighting people?'

'Art,' Carter said, taking a sip of his beer, 'is a psychopath, pure and simple. He is the self-professed returned King Arthur, and he set up the compound himself back in the 1980s.'

'You can't have been there for that long, you don't look that old?' Melissa said.

'No.' Carter smiled. 'I joined in 2012 and left two years ago.'

'So you believe this Art to be a psychopath?' Sister Veronica said, leaning over to check on Hope. 'My, this baby is having a good sleep. Probably means she's going to keep me up all night. That's a strong word to label another human being, Carter. Are you sure?'

'It's not a strong enough word, Sister.' Anger flashed through Carter's eyes. 'If you knew what I do, you'd understand.'

'Tell me then,' Sister Veronica said gently, smiling up at one of Carter's friends, who was placing a fresh drink in front of her. 'What's this, it smells like elderflower juice?'

'It's elderflower champagne,' the friend said. 'A speciality round here. Try it, it's amazing.'

'Well, I don't know...' Sister Veronica raised the glass dubiously to her lips. 'I usually only have one glass of eggnog on Christmas day.'

'Oh, Sister, you have to try it,' Melissa said, putting down her own glass. 'It's so soft and fruity, hardly tastes alcoholic at all.'

Sister Veronica sipped her drink and smiled.

'Yes, you're right, it's delicious,' she said. 'Sorry, Carter, do go on.'

'Art – or King Arthur – as he seems to genuinely believe he is, was accused of abusing one of the girls there, Mona Adkins.'

Sister Veronica jolted forward, and Melissa put her drink down.

'Who accused him?' Sister Veronica asked.

'Mona did, herself. Up until that point, I'd really enjoyed my time at New Avalon. There was a great community spirit and everyone worked very hard on the land. I made some good friends there. But as the years went by, I noticed a change in Art's attitude towards me. At first he'd been so welcoming, so loving. He really seemed to believe in me, and it was something I needed as I've never known my own father. He made me, and all the other new recruits, feel special, you know?'

Sister Veronica nodded.

'Then what happened?'

'Then bit by bit, it seemed as though I wasn't good enough for him anymore. He started telling me I was lazy, that I needed to get a job and start paying money into New Avalon, instead of living off his land like a leech. So I did, got a job in Wells as a waiter in a restaurant, and gave all my earnings to Art, like everyone did. Then one night there was a big showdown during a meeting. Art's very big on loyalty and honour, and he doesn't like people talking about him behind his back. Mona, who'd been born at the cult, hadn't been happy for a while. She'd lost a lot of weight, and people were worried that she was on drugs like her mum.'

'What happened to her mother?'

'Died from a drug overdose a while back. Drugs used to be acceptable at the cult, LSD was actually encouraged as Art said if you take it with the right intentions it can open your mind. But people started taking too much of it, and smoking so much dope they forgot to come to meetings. When Lance got hooked on cocaine Art forbade anyone else from touching the stuff. Anyway, Mona's father left when she was small, had a falling out with Art and hasn't been seen since. Art has a way of pulling people into the centre of meetings and humiliating them if he's not happy. He calls it justice, but it's really horrible to watch. You aren't allowed to have any privacy at New Avalon,

Art wants to know what you are thinking, feeling and doing at all times. He said it was for our own good. Anyway, Mona had been making it known that she wanted to leave. She kept telling people that Art was a fraud, and this made a lot of people angry with her as they really trusted Art. Most of all it made Art livid, which is why he shamed her that night at the meeting. Started telling everyone to look at the mess she was, how weak and ugly she was becoming. Then Mona suddenly shouted, "Yeah, well that's your fault, isn't it? If you'd kept your hands to yourself all these years maybe I wouldn't be so fucked up". No one could believe it, but yet most of us knew it was true, just from looking at her standing and shaking in front of Art, her face as white as a ghost. Mona told everyone how he'd first raped her when she was eleven, and had carried on since then.'

Sister Veronica shook her head sorrowfully.

'Crikey,' Melissa said. 'What did Art say?'

'It's not often that Art loses his cool,' Carter said, taking another sip of beer. 'But that night he started ranting and raving, calling Mona a liar and a whore, saying how dare she accuse King Arthur of such an immoral act. But then his son Lance – Lancelot – joined in and said he knew it was true because he'd walked in once and saw his father holding Mona down while he raped her.'

Sister Veronica drew a breath in sharply.

'The poor, poor girl,' she said, her face grave.

'Art went ballistic at that point and banished Lance and Mona from the hall, saying they'd chosen the path to hell and that they could rot there for all he cared. By banishment he meant for them to go to one of the punishment huts on the edge of the compound. But by morning they'd packed up and left.'

'I don't blame them,' Melissa said grimly.

'I've come to realise New Avalon is a cult,' Carter said,

exhaling. 'I'm doing an online psychology degree now and I've read a lot about them.'

'Good for you,' Sister Veronica said.

'Art has all the classic traits of a cult leader,' Carter went on. 'He's good at love-bombing and gaining the trust of his followers. Feeding them his own version of the history of King Arthur, making people believe he is a God-like figure. Encouraging paranoia in the group, brainwashing people to put their whole lives in his hands, telling them what to think and punishing them if they step out of line. I couldn't see it when I was there though.'

'Is that why you left? Because of Mona?' Sister Veronica said.

'Yes,' Carter said. 'Like I mentioned, I was having doubts before that, but that was the last straw. It was weird, after listening to Mona I suddenly saw Art for who he really is, a dangerous, abusive fake who preys on people, sucking the life out of them. I still can't believe I bought into that place.' He looked down.

'You were right, Sister,' Melissa said with a sigh. 'New Avalon is a much darker place than their webpage shows.'

Carter snorted with laughter.

'That load of rubbish? Makes it look like a cross between *The Waltons* and a *National Geographic* documentary.'

Sister Veronica smiled.

'Did other people leave, too, after Mona told them the truth about Art?'

'Yes,' Carter said. 'Although some die-hard followers stayed. Morgana's the worst, she's a nightmare. Totally loyal to Art and won't hear a bad word said about him. Celeste, Mona's sister, is a die-hard follower too. She'll never leave that place.'

'Yes, we met her earlier today. It's really quite fortuitous that we bumped into you, Carter,' Sister Veronica said, accepting her second glass of elderflower champagne. 'Because we are actually trying to find Mona. That little baby over there,' she gestured towards the pram, 'is actually hers. And she seems to have disappeared. I don't suppose you know anything about her whereabouts?'

'The last thing I heard, from a friend of a friend, was that she's working as a prostitute in London.' Carter shifted position. 'But if she's disappeared from there, I'd look at Art. Talk about venting spleen, he was incensed, so venomous in his attacks on her after she'd left. Kept saying she was pure evil and would go up in flames in hell, and that if she didn't he would hunt her down and set her on fire himself.'

'Did he now?' Sister Veronica sat back, stroking her chin.

'I'll just check on Hope.' Melissa stood up, draining her glass.

Sister Veronica was just mulling over Carter's last words and wondering how it had got so dark without her noticing, when Melissa's scream ricocheted around the garden. In one movement she was on her feet.

'Hope?' Melissa's whole body was trembling as she bent down to search frantically around the pram. 'Sister, the baby's not here. She's gone.'

18

'Sorry?' Art said, unable to believe the words coming from the doctor's mouth. 'What did you say?'

He was standing in a small room in St Francis' Hospital. It had taken him two and a half hours to drive from New Avalon to South London in one of the commune's shared cars; he'd probably broken the speed limit a few times on the way there but it was better than waiting around, bored, behind slow drivers. Art couldn't abide anyone getting in his way, or stopping or delaying his actions when he'd decided to do something. And now he was standing in a waiting room like an idiot, because for some reason they weren't letting him see his son. Before the doctor arrived the nurse had asked him to sit down, but he'd refused. It was a sparse area, just three chairs and a utilitarian sofa, a side table and a bland picture of yellow flowers on the wall.

'I'm so sorry, Mr Pendragon,' the doctor standing opposite him repeated. 'But your son, Lancelot, died this morning. We were trying to get hold of next of kin to let them know, but we couldn't find a number for you.'

'No,' Art said. 'That's not possible. I've come to see him.

Look–' He brandished the box of chocolates he'd bought at a petrol station on the way. 'I need to give him these.' The decision to get them had been a hasty one. He never usually showed love to those who'd hurt him. But if there was any way he could get through to his firstborn, persuade him to come back to New Avalon so Art and the other knights could nurse him back to health and help set him back on the path towards salvation, then he would take it. He'd thought the time would be right, now that Lance was so vulnerable.

'I can see this is a real shock for you, and I'm sorry to have to break such bad news, Mr Pendragon,' the doctor said. 'We did everything we could, but Lancelot is dead.'

The realisation that this was the truth hit Art in the face like a ten-ton truck. His stomach lurched and a wave of anger overtook him. He sat down. Stupid boy. It was his own fault. Art couldn't count the amount of times he'd told Lance to stay away from drugs. The problem was, he never listened.

'Why?' he said. 'What happened? I thought he was doing okay?'

'He was showing positive signs to start with.' The doctor sat down on the chair opposite. 'He was responding well to treatment. To be honest, I wasn't expecting things to deteriorate so rapidly. He'd overdosed on a cocktail of drugs–'

Art shook his head.

'But his underlying health was stable and he was young, two important factors in recovery.'

'So why did he die?'

'To be absolutely honest, Mr Pendragon, we're not sure at the moment,' the doctor said. 'We have not been able to find a probable cause so far, so the coroner has ordered a post-mortem examination to take place, to rule out possible misadventure, or anything else.'

Art put his head in his hands. This was bad news. His son's

death unexplained; what if this in some way drew people's attention back to him and New Avalon again? The last thing he needed was any more bad associations with the place. If the police came sniffing around they'd cause trouble, unsettle his followers. No, he didn't need that.

'I know this is hard for you,' the doctor said, standing up. 'Please, stay here as long as you need. Take your time, the nurse will look after you.'

I'm not going to tell anyone about Lance, Art decided, his eyes shut tight. *Maybe Morgana, but no one else, not even Celeste. If he's gone anyway then there's nothing I can do. No one needs to know.* He sat there, curled over in the foetal position in the chair, for five minutes. The nurse came and sat quietly in a chair near him.

Then Art uncurled, stood up, stretched his limbs, chucked the box of chocolates in the nearby bin, and walked out of the room, without saying a word.

19

The owner of The Chocolate Berry called the police, while everyone who'd been sitting in the garden and café joined in with the search. Melissa had gone back out onto the high street, and was running up and down, staring into any buggies and prams that she saw, looking at people's arms to see if they were carrying anything, staring under every car, into all the cars, shouting for help, her voice strained and desperate. Sister Veronica, numb with shock and panic, kept searching round the garden, the toilets, and inside the building, going to the same places, staring at the same people many times. If she looked harder, better, she would find her. Listening out for a gurgle, a coo, a cry, anything. But it was too noisy, too much background din.

'She must be here somewhere,' she kept saying, over and over again. 'She must be. Please, God. Help me find her.'

Blue flashing lights swerved to a halt next to the fence, and within seconds two police officers were introducing themselves, assessing the situation, calling for backup, and questioning Sister Veronica and Melissa about what had happened, their manner calm and reassuring. But they were being too slow.

Sister Veronica almost screamed at them about this, restraining herself at the last minute. *Hurry up, stop talking into radios and asking questions. Just find the baby NOW.* She knew there was a protocol, that they were the professionals, but surely their careful investigative attitude was wasting time?

It was hard to tell exactly who noticed the fire first. But amid the chaos in the garden a shout went up:

'The building over there is on fire. Look, Goddess World is on fire. Someone dial 999.' A plethora of people got out their phones and began dialling.

Although distracted into a frenzied state by the ice-cold panic that had electrified her brain since Hope's disappearance, Sister Veronica turned towards the building she and Melissa had been in only hours before, just diagonally up the hill from the café. The fence in front of her was low, allowing a sufficient view.

A river of orange-red flames had already engulfed half the top floor of the building. Immense clouds of black smoke rose into the air, visible against the dark sky. The flames billowed upwards, the haste at which the fire spread was terrifying. Higher and higher it climbed, spanning out like a series of giant flaming peaks that soon consumed the rest of the top floor. It billowed out through the now desecrated roof like a scene from a horror film. The adjoining shop roofs were also smoking with flames creeping on to their exteriors. A loud bang inside the building prompted a ground-floor window to explode outwards, with smaller flames soon licking through the open space. The fact that it had all happened so quickly seemed impossible, yet it had. The evidence was in front of her sore eyes.

Sister Veronica stepped back. Much to her horror, what she saw in front of her was almost the exact image from the Destruction card placed on Hope, that also turned up in

Celeste's tarot reading. Melissa arrived next to her, tears streaming down her face.

'This is like a nightmare,' she said, anguish filling her voice. 'Why is the building on fire? It happened so quickly, I had no idea. Oh, Sister, we must find Hope.'

The police officers that had been asking them questions had disappeared. Everyone else who'd been helping them search was now distracted by the horrific spectacle in front of them, or had gone to help. With furnace-like heat radiating towards the café from the fire, Sister Veronica and Melissa continued looking under tables, in corners, under hedges, behind plants, barging their way through small groups, suspicious of everyone, staring at their arms and their bags, trying to ask if they'd seen anyone take a baby from their pram.

The unmistakeable wail of fire engines filled the air.

'Everybody out,' a male voice shouted, seconds later. 'This area is not safe. We're evacuating all the buildings near the fire. Everybody out!'

'We can't go,' Sister Veronica shouted at the fireman who was walking towards her. 'We need to find the baby. Someone's taken the baby.' Her voice was a scream. 'All the Saints in Heaven, can't someone help us?'

One of the police officers was running back towards her.

'Come with me,' she said, taking hold of Sister Veronica's shaking hand, half pulling, half dragging her towards the gate. Melissa grabbed the pram and followed.

The scene they ran into on the high street, Sister Veronica reflected later, was like Armageddon. Falling debris, charred fragments floating down, firemen battling the blaze, with some pushing people back and shouting for them to leave. Three fire engines parked haphazardly, police cars behind them. And the heat, oh the temperature was unbearable, like being roasted alive in an oven.

'Does anyone have any reason to be in there that you know of?' a fireman shouted to the crowd, now further down the street. 'We need to get them out if they're in there, the building's about to collapse.'

Several people shouted back saying the shop was closed and the upper rooms were just used for storage of stock and tarot readings, that no one actually lived there.

As a fireman ushered her party along, she saw three more firemen run out of the burning door of Goddess World at the same time as loud cracks pierced the night. The entire first floor of the building was collapsing, crashing down, causing a new wave of fizzing flames, smoke and debris to shoot out.

'Couldn't find anyone,' she heard one of them say. 'But we couldn't get up the stairs. They'd already burnt away.'

'I'll take you to the police station,' the police officer said as they ran towards the cooler – still smoky – air away from the fire. 'I'm going to do everything I can to help you find the baby. I'm going to need you to tell me as much information as possible.'

But how can anyone do anything amidst this carnage? Sister Veronica's brain felt like it was splitting, fragmenting, as she walked down the street with the policewoman. *How on earth are we going to find Hope? She was snatched, I'm sure of it. But by who? Who would do that? Oh, God, please help us now.*

20

Dr Abaeze Obademi, pathologist at St Francis' Hospital, rubbed his forehead as he stared at the laptop in front of him. He was tired, he'd already been at the hospital for thirteen hours. His patient wife would have covered his plate of cold food, he thought, and gone to bed by herself, as usual. Maybe one day they would actually get to spend the evening together. He'd written so many similar reports over the last few months, and it was sad to write another. Depressing. He couldn't help imagining how he'd feel if this was his own son, how devastated a family somewhere was right now. He sighed.

Mr Lancelot Pendragon, he began to type.

Having met with attending doctors prior to the examination of Mr Lancelot Pendragon, I ascertained that the patient had been admitted to intensive care at St Francis' Hospital following a self-administered polydrug overdose. After initially responding to treatment and showing signs of improvement, he was found dead by a nurse on the morning of the date stated above. Although every effort was made by hospital staff to resuscitate Mr Pendragon, he was pronounced dead at 9.46am that day.

I was asked to perform a post-mortem examination directly, for the purposes of verifying the fact of his death.

At approximately 4.30pm on the day of examination, photographs of the body were taken under my direction.

I examined the body myself, and noticed that rigor mortis was fully established in all muscle groups.

The primary pattern of hypostasis was entirely within the posterior with blanching over the mid-back and buttocks.

There were no signs of forced injury marks on the body.

His liver and kidneys were found to be in various states of deterioration at the time of his death.

At the time of writing this report I have just been informed by Dr Timothy Sewell from the toxicology lab of the results from the blood sample taken from the body.

In summary, it is my opinion that the main factors involved in bringing about the death of Lancelot Pendragon were the high levels of methylenedioxy, cocaine, morphine, amphetamine, methamphetamine and cannabis found in his blood, still

```
present two days after his admission to
hospital, and the subsequent oxygen
starvation of his liver and kidneys.
    Manner of death: accidental polydrug
overdose.
```

Well there we go, Dr Obademi thought, clicking the send button. *No misadventure here, just a sad, predictable result to add to the rest of the rising statistics.* His email, with the post-mortem report attached, whizzed away through cyberspace to the inbox of the coroner.

21

'The first twenty-four hours will be the most critical,' Detective Inspector Yvonne Harding was saying. A stout, middle-aged woman who looked like she rarely smiled, Sister Veronica couldn't help wondering if she'd have the maternal instinct necessary to really give power to the search for Hope. Surely the nice PC Matharu, the officer who had guided Sister Veronica away from The Chocolate Berry, and had introduced her to the detective on their arrival at the police station, would be better? She'd said she had children of her own, that this was every parent and carer's worst nightmare. Her compassion had caused fresh outbursts of tears for both Melissa and herself. DI Harding wasn't wearing a wedding ring, she didn't look like the nuclear family type. More of a lone wolf, a dispassionate hunter of criminals. But not necessarily a lover of babies. 'Like I said, I'm going to do everything I can to help you, one step at a time. I do understand how worrying this is, but try and keep clear heads. In cases like this the child is usually found safe and well relatively quickly. Firstly, is there anyone you can call, anyone at all, who you think might have taken the baby?'

Sister Veronica and Melissa stared at each other, their faces ashen-grey and exhausted.

'Mona,' Melissa said. 'We've been looking for the baby's mother. That's why we came to Glastonbury in the first place.' She gave DI Harding a brief rundown of events.

'Right, I'm going to make some phone calls,' the detective said, staring at her. 'Stay here, I won't be long.' She left the room.

Sister Veronica stayed still, her mind disintegrating with worry and fear, feeling like she was on the escalator to hell. Melissa paced the room, tears running down her face.

A few minutes later, DI Harding returned.

'I've spoken to my colleagues at the Met and they've confirmed they haven't found Mona yet. So it could be her who took Hope, but we need to keep all our options open. Anyone else that you can think of?'

Sister Veronica explained about Celeste, their visit to her earlier that day, her surprise at being an aunt, her connections with New Avalon. DI Harding's face darkened when she heard the name of the commune.

'Right, so *they* could be involved. That lot are bad news. They've been on my radar for a while.'

'Don't you think it's a bit of a coincidence,' Melissa said to her, 'that we visited Celeste in Goddess World, and now it's burning down and her niece has gone? I mean, I don't know how those things can be connected but it just seems too close to be a complete accident.'

'We are going to look into all leads as thoroughly as possible,' DI Harding said. 'I can't give you an answer about that at the moment, but we will be investigating all possible connections. Can you think of any other relevant information you can tell me?'

Sister Veronica explained that the men she'd spoken to in

Soho had told her about someone shouting up at Mona's flat, asking for Lance, who they believed to be Mona's new partner.

'Is Lance the father of the baby?' DI Harding said.

'We're not sure,' Melissa said. 'It seems Mona led a very complicated life. No one seems to know who Hope's father is.'

DI Harding took them through the events leading up to Hope's disappearance in great detail, making notes all the time. Asking if Hope had any noticeable marks on her body that would help identify her if they found a baby – Sister Veronica told her about the island-shaped birthmark on the baby's thigh. Melissa told her about the green-and-yellow outfit Hope had worn all that day. Then they spoke about Celeste in more detail, about how they'd ended up in The Chocolate Berry, how by chance they'd met an ex-member of New Avalon, Carter, who'd been able to give them much more information about Mona and the abuse she'd suffered at the hands of their leader – the apparently returned King Arthur.

'I'll build a list of everyone who was at The Chocolate Berry while you were,' she said when they'd finished. 'If Hope was lying sleeping in her pram right next to the fence, and you were distracted, chatting and drinking – what was it?'

'Elderflower champagne.' Melissa looked down. Why oh why had they drunk it? They'd been too relaxed, taken their eye off the ball, and now look what had happened. Could Carter and his friends have been getting them drunk on purpose, could it have been them who had taken Hope? *Yes*, she thought. *That was a definite possibility.*

'Ah yes, elderflower champagne,' DI Harding said. 'Then someone seems to have taken advantage of the darkening evening, leaned over, and removed the baby from the pram without you or anyone else noticing. From what you've told me, there's several people of interest we need to speak to, particularly Carter and his friends. And I'll be phoning your convent too, Sister, to see if anyone there knows anything, or has heard anything. We need to cover all bases very thoroughly.'

Sister Veronica's already ragged, broken heart plummeted further down.

'Of course,' she said. This would be the end of her, and quite right too, she reflected. Mother Superior would never forgive her. It was entirely her fault; what had she been thinking, swanning off to Glastonbury with the baby, drinking champagne, for goodness' sake, and not checking enough on Hope? And to think, her stupidity had caused such an awful thing to happen. Sick with guilt, she could barely meet the detective's gaze.

'Don't be too hard on yourself,' DI Harding said, as though she was a mind reader. 'You haven't done anything wrong, Sister. And you are doing everything in your power now to help us find Hope, working with me and telling me everything helpful that you know. What you really need to do is go and get some rest, go back to your guest house now and try and get some sleep. Trust that my colleagues and I will be doing everything in our powers to find the little girl while you're there. I've got Melissa's number and I'll get in contact with you the minute we hear something.'

But as Sister Veronica and Melissa left the police station – that was nestled in a cul-de-sac at the bottom of Glastonbury High Street – their shoulders sagging, the pram now taken by the police as evidence, Sister Veronica stopped and shook her head.

'There's no way I can go back to the guest house and sleep now,' she said, her voice dull and monotone. 'You go, Melissa, you look tired. I'm going to carry on searching for Hope.'

'Are you bloody joking?' Melissa wiped her nose with the back of her sleeve, her eyes flashing with anger. 'I'm not going anywhere. Do you really think I could sleep knowing the baby's gone? I know I haven't spent as much time with Hope as you, but

I really care about that child. I'm going to keep looking too. Maybe we should split up, we can cover more ground that way?'

Sister Veronica nodded. They agreed that Melissa would search the back roads around Glastonbury town centre, the ones full of terraced and semi-detached houses with tie-dye drapes and wind chimes in their windows, and Sister Veronica would concentrate on the main streets – or as much of them as she could get to, given the calamity of the fire that had destroyed Goddess World. It was worth looking in the most unlikely places, they decided. In bins, doorways, cars, porches, anywhere and everywhere that may be big enough to hold or hide a baby.

Sister Veronica trudged back up the hill, past shops and cafés still glowing in the light of the dying fire. She went slowly, stopping to examine even the smallest object in detail, staring distrustfully at anyone she saw, trying to establish whether they were hiding anything.

What if we never find her? she reflected, torturing herself. She stopped walking, feeling hysteria rise within her. *No, Veronica,* she shouted at herself. *You will NOT do this now, allow your stupid emotions to hamper your search for Hope. Stop it, stop it now. And carry on looking for as long as it takes. This is your fault, so you can fix it without giving in to a maudlin frenzy.*

Steadying herself for a moment or two, waving black smoke from in front of her face, Sister Veronica walked on. She would stay awake for a night, a week, do whatever was necessary. She was going to make things right. She was going to find Hope.

22

Gareth Pendragon, alone in his hut, pulled his khaki rucksack from under his camp bed. Into it went clean underwear and socks, a jumper, T-shirt, trousers, his best knife, a bottle of water, his wallet, phone, charger and laptop. He now knew what he needed to do, and he needed to start it right away.

He hadn't meant to overhear his father's phone conversation with the hospital; he'd actually been going to Art's study to see if they could discuss his ideas about the new webpage. Gareth loved technology and had taught himself to use some new software he thought would really make a difference; help present New Avalon in a much more modern, appealing way. His father seemed to have forgiven him for his transgressions, and Gareth was now allowing his arm to heal. But as he'd approached the closed study door in his father's large hut – the grandest on site – he'd heard his father talking on the phone. Creeping closer until he was right next to the door, he held his breath, his ear close to the door. He'd discovered many titbits of information in the same way over the years.

'So Lancelot died from an accidental drug overdose?' His father's voice sounded calm. Almost relieved. Hearing those words caused dizziness to overtake Gareth but he knew if he made a sound and was discovered Art would make sure his life wasn't worth living. 'Are you sure?'

There was a pause.

'Okay, okay,' his father said a minute or two later. 'Thank you for letting me know the cause of death.'

Gareth stole away, having heard enough. His beloved, traitorous brother was dead. And he hadn't had a chance to say goodbye or make things right after Lance's sudden departure from home. His father had made sure he hadn't, he was good at that sort of thing; the one time Gareth made it to London, his father had found out and been furious.

But now he was going to make Art proud, he was going to do something that would help soothe his father's pain.

The truth was that he had a secret that not even King Arthur knew about. And now, hearing about Lance, he found he suddenly had enough wild energy to see it through.

A splinter of fear dug into his insides and he chastised himself for being a wimp and a coward. No, that was the old Gareth, he told himself. The new one was as brave as the knight he really was. Acting fast would quell the ounce of dread in him, he thought, the weak side of him he'd always allowed to rule his choices before. When Lance had lived at New Avalon he'd always been the daredevil out of the two of them, always ready to be spontaneous and take chances. Gareth remembered the time when Lance climbed onto the roof of the Great Hall when his father was up at the town. 'Come up here and join me,' he'd shouted down to his brother. 'Come on, you'll love it.' But Gareth had smiled and shook his head, fearing the fall. Well, no more. He was ready to be spontaneous and take chances now. He imagined Lance's spirit egging him on. 'Come on, Gareth, you can do it. Don't be a chicken.'

'I *am* going to do it,' Gareth said out loud.

He pulled the drawstring on his bag tight, rammed his hat down over his ears, threw on his coat and put his torch in his pocket. He stepped out into the crisp September night air, looked around, and made his way quietly to the hole in the compound fence.

23

'I can't find her anywhere, Art,' Bedivere was saying, his voice sounding strained and tired. He and the rest of the New Knights at New Avalon had spent the night and day searching for Celeste. Art had shouted at them, ranted, hit people – he'd smacked Bedivere on the jaw so hard it was now red and swollen – thrown things around, but still his favourite mistress, his obsession, had not, and could not, be found. Bedivere knew they had a low chance of finding her if him and his group went out again, but contradicting his incensed king right now would be tantamount to suicide.

'It was a bad fire,' Morgana soothed. 'I went up and saw the remains of Goddess World today while I was looking for her, it's all gone, just a ruin now. Still smoking. She's probably just upset, Art. Her workplace has just burned down and you know she doesn't do well with trauma. Remember how she used to go and hide in places after her mother died – it took her nearly a year to start joining in with life here again. She nearly stopped speaking at one point. To be honest, I reckon Celeste's probably gone off somewhere to clear her head.' She was surprised at the strength of her king's reaction. She knew he adored the girl, but his current fury was on another level; it was primal, it was like watching a lion go mad and destroy its habitat. It had been a surprise to her when the girl had vanished, totally unexpected and out of character. But if need be, Morgana had ways and means of finding people; research was what she excelled at. She would just need some time.

'I want her here now,' Art roared. 'Find her, you useless bunch of lazy bastards. Don't tell me you've already looked for her, I know what you're like. You just want to go to bed, you're being selfish and unhelpful, the lot of you. GO NOW AND DON'T COME BACK UNTIL YOU'VE FOUND HER OR GOD WILL SMITE YOU ALL.' Art's world was spiralling out of control. First Lance died, his poor, stupid son – he'd still only told Morgana about him – and now Celeste couldn't be found. This, in many ways, was worse than Lance's demise because Celeste had been *his*. He'd made sure of it. He'd wanted her so badly and he'd got her, shaped her, moulded her into how he wanted her to be. She was such a good girl, always willing to please, and her eyes. Oh how he melted when she looked at him sometimes. She was exciting, different from the other more chilled-out women at the compound, who seemed happy to get on with domestic life quietly. But Celeste wasn't like that, she had more spark. And her heart belonged to him. And she'd always been faithful and loyal, *always*. She'd never disappeared before. She knew he needed to know where she was at all times and she'd honoured that in the past. He owned her, she owed her life to him. He'd looked after her well after her mother died, treated her like a princess, made sure she'd wanted for nothing. But where the hell was she now? Why would she go anywhere? Why would she need to? She loved New Avalon almost as much as he did. It just didn't make sense. Maybe she had been caught in the fire? Maybe something horrific had happened to her? That was an awful thing to contemplate. Feeling powerless made Art enraged, helplessness was not a feeling he could deal with, it could not be tolerated on any level. He'd structured his life to limit that happening. But now this. He roared again.

Bedivere's shoulders were drooping, his eyes smarting with exhaustion. Since Celeste had failed to come home after her day's work, Art had ordered him to head up the search for her so he'd personally looked in every hut on the compound, had teams out searching the woodland, orchards and fields. He'd gone to all the places he thought Celeste might like, driven one of the compound's communal cars around for hours until it was running on fumes. But no luck. The girl had apparently vanished, or maybe didn't want to be found. He personally didn't really see what the big deal was, she'd probably come back when she was ready. He'd sent a separate group to retrace Celeste's steps in Glastonbury Town with instructions to be as thorough as possible, leave no stone unturned and all that. But, of course, when they'd got there they'd found they couldn't reach Goddess World itself, because by then the high street was totally blocked at both ends. It had been chaos by all accounts, police cars, fire engines and ambulances all over the place. So, instead, the group had stayed staring at the inferno of flames tearing up into the sky, calling Art on his mobile to report on matters, and fearing the worst about Celeste, before going back to face the wrath of their leader.

Knowing from experience that resistance to Art's instructions was pointless, Bedivere turned and indicated to the group of hollow-eyed knights to turn and leave the hall, which they did without protest. Morgana was the only one who didn't move.

For a moment she looked as though she was about to say something, then she paused.

'Can I give you a hug?' she said a few seconds later, opening her arms invitingly to Art. 'If I'm honest you look like you need one.'

'NO, you cannot give me a FUCKING HUG.' Art's face was red as he spun towards her, a vein throbbing at the side of his forehead, sweat stains on his tunic. 'If you want to help me, go and find CELESTE, woman. For God's sake stop pissing about in here wasting my time. Go and be useful for once in your life.'

Morgana turned and headed for the door. Even in her absence, all he thought about was that bloody girl, she thought. How was she supposed to know where Celeste had gone? She'd always done her best to atone to Art's wishes that she act like a mother figure to Celeste, and also to Mona when she was still at New Avalon. So Morgana had done her best, taught them the principles of Art's manifesto – loyalty, honour and integrity – brought them up to be the best New Knights that she could. They'd called her Auntie Morgs. She'd failed with Mona, but Celeste had always shone like a jewel, loved by everybody at the compound. She was light where her sister was dark. She was a bit too conceited, in Morgana's opinion, a bit too aware of her own beauty and feminine wiles to be truly attractive. And the spell she'd cast on Art was sickening to behold. Who would have thought he would take news of her absence in such a way? Morgana shut the door behind her more loudly than she normally would.

Art picked up a chair and hurled it across the room. It hit the bookcase, causing many of the remaining items that hadn't already been thrown across the room to come crashing down. Volumes of socialist ranting, stacks of old video tapes – he loved to watch himself pontificating to a crowd – all sorts of presents and mementoes from his New Knights, a photo of Celeste looking ravishing in her golden dress, pots full of pens and pencils, unposted letters to MPs and other prominent figures, and several papers full of his writings soon littered his floor. He stamped across the debris, uncaring.

Why was this happening to him? Why was God punishing him? Surely he'd shown his loyalty to the Almighty, followed the dreams and visions he'd had to the best of his ability?

Insane thoughts swirled through Art's mind. Someone was behind all this. Punishment was being brought upon New Avalon because someone in the compound was unclean, and was up to no good. Someone had fallen so far from grace that the Almighty had stepped in and was trying to warn Art before anything else happened. That somebody needed to be cleansed and purified right away, to save New Avalon. And suddenly, with absolute clarity, God planted that person's name in his head: Lucan. Lucan Butler.

24

Sister Veronica and Melissa collected their drinks from the side of the counter, and sank onto the hard bistro-style chairs. Neither of them had slept, and Hope was still nowhere to be found. Today they'd chosen The Blue Gecko café for sustenance. It was a small establishment, and more of a run-of-the-mill type café inside rather than the fairy-tale experience created by The Chocolate Berry, but one of the only places still open – the fire had caused a great deal of the high street's trading places to remain shut and off limits.

Melissa had started smoking again, and she'd got through one and a half packets already since the previous night. Two of her fingers were already stained a faint yellow from the nicotine, which Sister Veronica considered to be a most ghastly sight. 'It's the stress,' Melissa had explained. 'I can't handle it, Sister.' Of course, she didn't blame her friend at all for the smoking, and found she actually didn't care. The only all-consuming thing on her mind was finding the baby.

Walking through the daylight remains of last night's fiery destruction had only echoed her inner feelings of devastation. What was left of Goddess World – a couple of walls and a pit of rubble – was still smoking, but at least the flames had gone. The buildings on either side of it were burnt to varying degrees, scorch marks covering a good deal of their facades. An impressive clean-up operation had already taken place on the pavements and road in front of the site, and several police officers and other officials were present, some sifting carefully through the wreckage, others discussing matters in low voices.

Sister Veronica stared out of the window. She felt desolate, empty, as though all the colour in the world had been sucked away. And she felt responsible. How could she not? She'd wanted Sister Catherine to ask her to bring Hope to Glastonbury, yearned for the responsibility of having the baby girl in her charge for a few days. And look what she'd done; accepted alcoholic drinks from people she didn't know, and not been vigilant enough to notice the baby's abduction. Shame didn't even touch the inner hatred she had for herself. She should have known better, but she hadn't. It was unforgiveable, what she'd done. For all she knew, that Carter and his friends may have had a hand in Hope's disappearance. Why had she trusted them? How could she have been so naïve and stupid?

'Why are the officers winding a line of blue-and-white tape in front of the building?' Her voice was flat, tired. A long-haired waiter, who'd been clearing mugs from a nearby table, turned round, his nose piercing glinting in the dull light.

'Apparently when the firemen could enter the building they found human remains,' he said. 'People round here have been talking about it all morning. Makes you sick, really, what happens to some people.'

'Do they know who it was?' Melissa said, immediately thinking of Celeste.

'No, the body was too badly burned, although I have heard they're pretty sure it was a female.' The waiter walked closer to them, balancing a tray. 'That's what people are saying, anyway.

Looks like the fire was deliberate, they've found several sites around the debris where they think blazes were intentionally started. I was back at New Avalon at the time, but some of my friends were here, and they said they couldn't believe how quickly the fire spread.'

'New Avalon?' Sister Veronica sat up, a minute amount of energy reappearing in her veins. If she could do anything to help find Hope, then she absolutely would, and New Avalon seemed like an excellent place to start, and speaking to a resident from the place was more than she could have hoped for. 'The King Arthur compound?'

'Yes.' The man's lips twitched into a smile. 'I've never heard it described quite like that, but you're right, it is designed around the theme of King Arthur, and the way we live is influenced by the history and legend surrounding him.'

Sister Veronica introduced herself and Melissa, and gave a quick summary of their reasons for being in Glastonbury; they were looking for a girl called Mona Adkins, her baby had been left on the convent's doorstep, they needed to find her to make sure she was okay and to see if they could reunite mother and daughter. It was Melissa who had to explain about how Hope had been taken the night before, Sister Veronica couldn't bring herself to say the words. The waiter's face immediately changed, his smile vanishing, replaced instead by an intense gaze.

'Do you mind if I sit down with you for a minute?' he asked, looking over his shoulder. The café was quiet, and no one was waiting at the counter.

'Please do,' Sister Veronica said, pulling out a chair for him. 'We're desperate for information, anything at all that could help us.'

'I'm Lucan,' the waiter said, sitting down. 'I've lived in New Avalon for getting on thirty years. I knew Mona well. *Really* well.'

Melissa watched him carefully.

'I hope you don't mind me asking,' she said. 'But were you guys ever together? As in, in a relationship? Something just now in the way you said that made me think you were.'

'Yes.' Lucan exhaled. 'Freedom of sex among adults at New Avalon is encouraged – sorry, Sister, but it is – but I always loved Mona the best out of all the girls. I know she was a lot younger than me, but we just clicked, you know? Talked for hours, all the way through the night sometimes. She was one of the most genuine people there, she had an honesty about her that was refreshing. She was a complex person as well, a tortured soul on the one hand, but so bright and funny on the other.'

'Did you know she was planning to leave?' Sister Veronica picked up her mug. 'We've heard about what happened to her, about the leader's abuse. Did you know what Art did to her before she told everyone at the meeting that night?'

'No.' Lucan sighed, shaking his head, his expression suddenly strained. 'I had no idea until she said it all that night. I wanted to kill Art when I found out. Still do, really. I couldn't believe he'd do that to her, and for so many years. What kind of monster abuses their position of trust and responsibility like that? I really wanted to see Mona after it all came out, check she was okay. But she'd vanished. I looked everywhere, I really did. Loads of us did. The next day we realised she and Lance had made a run for it. Turned out, from the amount they'd packed, that they must have been planning to go for a while. They couldn't have got their things together so thoroughly in just one evening.'

'Have you seen her since?' Melissa took a sip of her large latte.

Lucan paused. He seemed to be deciding whether or not to answer.

'Yes,' he said, finally. 'I have seen her, but I've never told a soul this, not even anyone at New Avalon. Not just to protect myself, but for Mona's benefit too.'

'Go on,' Sister Veronica said softly, leaning forwards. *At last, more information*, she thought. *Thank goodness we met you, Lucan.*

'I-I missed her so much.' Tears came to Lucan's eyes. 'I really did love the girl, she was so special, and I thought she had feelings for me, from the way she acted. It really hurt when she left, I felt like I'd been dumped – though we're not supposed to have strictly monogamous relationships at New Avalon. But sometimes you can't help it, it's human nature. But even so, last year I decided to go and find her, to talk things over with her, make sure she was okay after everything that had happened. And to be honest, I also wanted to see if there was a chance of us being together, somehow.'

Melissa and Sister Veronica both nodded, understanding.

'I'd heard she was working as a prostitute in Soho,' Lucan said. 'Word gets around, you know, we're not as cut off from the outside world in the commune as people seem to think. And this broke my heart. Mona was too precious to do that kind of work, to sell her body. But I think Art had broken her self-esteem, made her feel worthless, you know, with all the abuse? Anyway, one day I told Art I was going on a retail trip for the café, but instead I actually took a day off and travelled up to London, and found her pretty quickly after asking around. We chatted for ages, and... er, I spent the night with her.'

'Did you sleep with her?' Melissa asked.

'Yes.' Lucan nodded. 'But the next day she told me to go. Said she had a client coming and that I mustn't be there when he arrived. I asked if we could keep in contact, and she gave me her phone number, but when I got home and tried to call her it didn't connect. Turns out she'd given me an old number that wasn't working. She obviously didn't want me in her life anymore. So I just left it. Until recently, when I suddenly got this feeling that I needed to find her again.'

'Why do you think that was?' Sister Veronica said, gazing at him.

'I don't know. Listen, this is really hard to explain and you guys will probably think I'm crazy. *I* think I'm crazy myself half the time.' Lucan's brow furrowed and he leant forwards, resting his elbows on his knees. 'Like I said, I've been at New Avalon for nearly thirty years now. I first joined because I needed to get out of mainstream society, away from all the people around me who only believed money and status were important, I found everything about that way of life shallow and soul-destroying. Arriving at New Avalon for the first time felt like coming home to me, I really felt like I belonged. When I found out Art really believed he was the returned King Arthur I didn't pay too much attention to it. It just seemed like another quirky, fun thing about the place, like make-believe. It took me a while to understand he was actually serious about it. The thing is, he uses his status as a king to rule New Avalon with utter control. He's spent so long telling us all about God, and what we need to do to get into heaven, and how easy it is for the Devil to get into our hearts. So much has happened over the years, and now I really don't know what to think. I kind of do believe what Art tells us about salvation, and I'm worried that because of the choices she's made, Mona may not be saved. She may not go to heaven when the time comes, she may have taken a dark and dangerous path by leaving the commune. And I really want to help her with that.'

Melissa stared at him with wide eyes. Sister Veronica reached forward and patted his knee. Then she sighed.

'I think I understand you, Lucan,' she said. 'I've been having a crisis of faith myself. For so long I believed everything I was taught in the Roman Catholic Church. I may not have been the best at following it, but I didn't question much, I trusted the people who guided me through and gave myself to God in the manner I was told. However, recently I've been finding out that several aspects of my church are a sham, and it's really thrown me into a spiritual quandary.'

Lucan gazed at her, his eyes bright.

'So you understand,' he said. 'How difficult beliefs can be. How they can play with your mind?'

'Yes,' Sister Veronica said quietly. 'I do. But one thing I've learned over the last few months, Lucan, and I want you to listen carefully to this; is that when other people around you are saying things that sound mad or unbelievable, don't give your power to them. Don't just follow their commands without question. Turn inwards and find your own truth, and listen to it. Because in my opinion, that's what's real.' She sat back.

'I think I understand what you're saying, Sister,' Melissa said slowly, flicking a strand of pink hair away from her coffee. 'If Lucan really believes Mona is going to hell because of her choices, then fine. But if he has doubts about that, and is only thinking that because it's what this Art has told him, then it's better for him to listen to his intuition.'

'Exactly.' Sister Veronica took a slurp of tea. 'That's exactly what I'm trying to get across.'

'Thank you.' Lucan ran his hands through his hair. 'It's lovely to hear a voice of reason for once. Everything Art says now makes me feel empty and confused. I think I've started to hate him. Is that terrible?'

'No, not at all,' Sister Veronica said gently. 'Sometimes we have to move away from people who were previously heroes to us if what they are doing or saying is harmful in some way, and there's nothing at all wrong with that. Oh yes, by the way,' she went on, suddenly remembering her worries, 'did you ever know someone called Carter, or what did he say his other name was? Oh yes, Lamorak, who used to live at New Avalon?'

'Yes, I knew Lamorak.' Lucan looked surprised. 'He was a nice fellow. Quiet. He left a few years ago, obviously more sensible than me. Why?'

'We met him yesterday in a café,' Melissa said. 'And he told us a bit about New Avalon and Mona. And about what sort of person Art is. We were wondering if he had anything to do with Hope's abduction, because we were talking to him when she went missing, and some of his friends were buying us drinks. After it all happened I wondered if we'd been duped by them, if his chatting to us was just a cover for his friends snatching the baby.'

'No, I wouldn't think so.' Lucan seemed shocked. 'Well, of course, it's hard to really know what goes on in anyone's mind, but he always seemed like a kind sort of person to me. No, I really don't think he'd be the sort to do anything like that.'

Sister Veronica sighed again. Perhaps there was no lead there then after all. Which was a good thing, but also left her feeling as helpless as before.

'I must ask you, Lucan,' she said seriously, turning to him as a thought occurred to her. Could they even trust the man sitting with them now? How did they know he was telling them the truth? At least one person who'd been in Glastonbury had snatched Hope away from them, and until they found out who that was she couldn't afford to trust anyone. '*Did* you ever get back in touch with Mona again?'

'No.' Lucan shook his head. 'The idea only occurred to me the other night. Actually, I've also been thinking about leaving New Avalon. Terrible things have been happening there.' A look of fear flashed through his eyes and he looked around, as though checking there was no one he knew listening to what he was saying. 'You wouldn't believe what goes on there even if I told you.'

'Don't worry,' Sister Veronica said, with kindness in her voice. 'No one can hear us. You can speak freely.'

'What kind of things?' Melissa said. 'We do believe you, Lucan. You don't have to worry about that.'

'Well, the latest thing,' Lucan said, checking behind himself again, 'is that Celeste didn't come home last night. Art's gone mad, literally. Been smashing up furniture, whacking people when they get in his way, honestly, I've never seen him like this before. He's usually so in control.'

The colour drained from Sister Veronica's face.

'And you say a female body was found in the burnt-out building?' Nausea rose through her. 'If she's missing that could surely be Celeste? Did they find any other bodies? Perhaps a smaller, baby-sized one?'

'Oh, Sister,' Melissa gasped. 'Do you really think that's what's happened?'

25

Gareth sat on a London Tube, hugging his secret to himself. He was trying to ignore the grimy smell around him, and the litter of crisp packets, tickets, newspapers and other rubbish strewn across the carriage floor. Externals were so messy sometimes. Gareth liked everything to be orderly and neat. He was wondering why he'd never taken steps to put his plan into action before, and he wasn't sure of the answer. He'd probably been too afraid to take such a big step, but hearing about Lance's death had changed all that. He knew he was doing this for his brother as well as for Art. His father's words kept going round in his head: *Do something that matters, Gareth. Something big. Make a stand, make me proud of you.* And so his plan had come to fruition in his mind. It must be God talking through him, he thought. And that was a wonderful thing. He'd been waiting for something like this to happen to him his whole life.

The idea had first floated into his head a while back, and had got stronger every time he'd listened to his father, King Arthur, talk about coming back to save Britain, about how the people here needed him. Gareth wasn't very clear on what his dad was actually doing to save the UK; he knew Art believed that writing was powerful, and that he spent many nights in his study penning letters to different public figures, telling them what they were doing wrong, and setting out clear protocols of behaviour they should follow in the future. He wasn't sure if any of them ever wrote back. He knew his father didn't agree with what he called 'the media machine', all the advertising aimed at young people, all the glitz and glamour promised if you bought certain magazines. But Art never seemed to do anything about that either. Gareth worried that it was because his father was too busy to take action, what with running New Avalon, which took up most of his time. He never seemed to undertake the bigger projects he talked about. If truth be told, he never really had time for Gareth either. The secret idea Gareth was finally going to put into action now would change all that.

Gareth knew a bigger step needed to be taken in New Avalon's fight against the evils in Britain – his father had talked about that a lot at meetings – and he'd saved for a long time in order to buy the train tickets he needed, worked extra hours at the phone-case stand in the high-street market. He had to give most of his earnings to his dad, of course, which was only right, how else would they run the commune if everyone didn't contribute? But he'd been keeping a few pennies back here and there, and at last he'd saved enough.

He knew one thing for sure, one thing his father had drummed into him over the years: King Arthur and the New Knights needed to rid Britain of her wicked ways. They needed to win the war against consumerism and capitalism, and bring her back to a more wholesome way of life. He'd heard his dad say so many times and it was frustrating that none of the other New Knights ever really did anything about this. He shifted position, looking up at the dark walls whizzing by outside the Tube carriage. Gareth liked the dark, it seemed to understand him. But that was wrong, darkness was where the Devil lived. He pulled back his sleeve and scratched his arm; punishing himself for bad thoughts. His father had always encouraged the New Knights to self-harm if they needed to atone for a wrongdoing. Creating a wound like that was a visual sign of your sin, he said. When it scabs, heals and goes, it means God has forgiven you.

Lancelot had let Art down very badly, and Gareth could see how much his death had hurt his father. Poor Lance, his beloved, stupid brother. Perhaps he took after their mother Shirley, she'd been weak too, his dad said. Gareth had never looked for her, never wanted to. His dad said he had everything he needed at New Avalon, and, as usual, he'd followed his words. He wouldn't fail Art like Lance had, no way. In fact, hearing that his brother was dead had finally given him the fire to leave, to go on his mission, to be the bigger, better person. He was the only son now, and he had to prove himself so that his father would really love him, finally sit up and take notice of him.

He hadn't eaten for several hours, but then he didn't need to. The gnawing feeling in his stomach would subside soon. As Art always said, God always provides for the true of heart, so Gareth knew God would look after him, he no longer needed food, as what he was doing was helping to fulfil his father's divine calling in a way Lance never had. He had water, that was all he'd need for now. What he was about to do would propel New Avalon into the public sphere, make people stop what they were doing and take notice of them for once; listen to their sound philosophies that were bound to bring salvation to the masses.

He imagined the proud beam on his father's face when he heard about what Gareth was about to do. Gareth wondered how the news would reach him. Maybe a television broadcast, he wondered. Tears may even come to his eyes, Gareth mused. Although to be honest, he'd never seen that happen before. But when Art knew what a true knight his one remaining son was, what a soldier, how devoted and loyal to the cause he was, he'd realise how much he loved him, Gareth was sure of it. He knew Art had always favoured Lance, he wasn't blind to that fact, never had been. But he'd change that very soon. Morgana would be thrilled too. Gareth imagined her enveloping him in one of her cosy hugs. Not for the first time, he wished she was his mother; Auntie Morgs was so warm, her kind words made everything feel okay. He'd never known his own mother, she'd left New Avalon when he was two, his father had said. Wasn't strong enough to conform to the tenets of loyalty, honour and integrity, apparently.

Pushing down his grief about the death of his brother that was making a hot craziness well up inside him, Gareth turned his attention to the adverts on the opposite wall, determined to let nothing put him off his course. He was halfway through reading about the birthplace of what purported to be the best whisky in the world, when the Tube suddenly slowed to a halt. The motion excited him, the whoosh echoed the manic energy building up inside him.

Ah good, it was his stop, Westminster. He swung his rucksack onto his shoulder, then stepped lightly out of the doors, listening to them whir shut behind him.

This was *his* calling, he felt sure of it. He may not be King Arthur, but knight and charger he most definitely was.

26

'Brothers and sisters, my precious New Knights,' Art spat. He'd been drinking all afternoon; whisky and mead, a potent combination when coupled with the unbridled anger, jealousy, grief and venom swilling around his mind. No one had been able to find Celeste, despite the constant searches. Morgana had informed him that Gareth had also left, taking some of his possessions with him. His one remaining heir. If his son had anything to do with Celeste's vanishing he would fucking kill him. The people gathered around him watched silently as he careered around the podium, exhaustion in their eyes – Art was making sure no one slept until Celeste was found – some mothers pulling their pale children closer to them. This was bad, they knew. Art's energy was palpable, it filled the room like one of the rampaging red dragons on the wall.

'It is a sin, a SIN, my friends, to go against me, to betray me. For by doing this you are turning your back against God the Almighty.' Sweat ran down Art's face, drops of it flicking onto other people as he turned this way and that. 'I have done all I can for you, shared my visions and dreams with you, pointed you on the path towards salvation. Many of you here are loyal;

you have shown me integrity and honour through your actions, and for that I thank you. You committed to this life, and you follow the rules.'

Morgana nodded, her hands clasped together in front of her bodice, her hair in a half ponytail. Awe and devotion shone in her eyes as she looked up at her king. She adored seeing him in full flow, with power oozing off him as he cast his spell over his followers. It was beyond attractive, she thought, the most primal masculine sexuality. She loved the way Art never reflected before he spoke, he didn't care what people thought of him. If he had a problem, then everyone knew about it. And tonight, he clearly had an issue he needed to get off his chest.

'But God has told me that one of you,' Art hissed. 'One of you is a traitor; a Judas Iscariot, a filthy pestilent disease amongst our ranks of purity. A malignant tumour spreading poison throughout our paradise.'

His followers looked around nervously at each other. Someone was in for big trouble that night and they were all hoping it wasn't them.

Art stepped forward and slapped Lucan so hard that his whole head turned sideways.

'He's not one of us,' Art said, looking around. 'He never has been. His betrayal has brought punishment on us from God. Hasn't it, Lucan?'

'Art,' Lucan said slowly, rubbing his jaw. 'I honestly don't know what you're talking about.'

'Liar,' Art whispered. 'You lay with the evil temptress, Mona.

You had sex with the fallen woman who is rotten at the core. She infected you with her abhorrent sin.'

'No.' Lucan shook his head. 'No, Art.'

'And you still lust after her now.' Art was so close that Lucan could smell the sourness of his breath. 'I've seen it in your eyes. You're as bad as she is. It's your fault Celeste's gone. The Almighty is punishing me for allowing you to live here, rotting us from the inside, tainting our purity with your wickedness.'

He slapped Lucan again, the harsh sound echoing round the hall.

Lucan turned back to face Art. He was still, silent.

'You slept with Mona too, Art.' When he spoke, his voice was low and steady. 'But you did it with force. You raped her, over and over again. And she hated every minute of it, she told us all that. So surely, by your own logic, you must also be infected by her? Be poisoned? In fact, I'm pretty sure God does not condone the kind of abuse you inflicted on her, so if any of us here are bringing punishment on New Avalon, then it's you, Art.'

'Brothers and sisters.' Art's anger was now on a new level; quiet and frightening, but there was a look of satisfaction in his eyes. He took a step back, away from Lucan, then looked around. 'Tell me now, as you stand before me, which one of you will not avenge this attack on your leader, King Arthur? Which one of you will condemn me to suffer with these words without taking vengeance on the Devil you see here before you? Tell me now, if I'm looking into your soul and talking about you.'

Silence.

'Tell me now if any of you are too weak to stand tall and save our beloved community from Satan?' Art went on, staring around.

Still silence, as though the assembled throng were holding a collective breath.

'I prayed long, and I prayed hard,' Art said. 'I asked God to give me an answer. Why were these things happening to his flock in New Avalon? Why did Mona act the way she did? Betraying my boy, Lancelot? Why have Celeste and Gareth now gone? Why is this misery upon us? Finally I received an answer: Lucan. Can you not see, friends, that we now have a way to save ourselves? To gain our rightful place in heaven once again? If we do as God asks, we will be spared. We must cleanse ourselves of Lucan's depravity once and for all and purify New Avalon. That is the will of the Lord.'

A murmur went through the New Knights.

'Step forward, any of you who stand with me,' Art said. 'Any of you who accept God's will, and who will aid the cleansing of our home. Any of you who really love one another enough to protect your family, and to safeguard the children who live with us from going to hell. Let me see who my most faithful followers are.'

Morgana was the first to step forward. Bedivere and a group of his friends followed soon after, all with apprehensive faces. This was bad, they knew. Something was going to be asked of them that they didn't want to do. But they'd have to submit to the will of their leader, like they had with Kay, and with others who'd been called out in meetings. Three young boys also walked into the centre of the hall.

'Sisters and brothers,' Art said. 'Through your loyalty you are earning your places as my most trusted allies. Come,' he turned to the mainly female remainers, 'who else? Do not let sensitivity cloud your decision. There is no room for uncertainty in God's plan. Do not forget, we are under attack. And as New Knights we must face this difficult time with honour.'

Slowly, the remaining crowd walked forward, one by one, until everyone, now in a straggling semi-circle, was standing in front of Lucan.

'Do not be scared.' Art smiled down at their faces. 'Cleansing ourselves will help save Lucan's blackened soul, it will give him another chance at redemption. Who amongst us wants him to reside in hell forever?'

More silence. Hardly any movement among the assembled throng. Everyone present seemed to be holding their breath, listening out for the next word from King Arthur's mouth.

'Lucan needs this. We all need this.' Art slurred his words, but his tone was light, encouraging. He'd changed tack, he was good at that. 'Look at me, knights. Trust in me, and trust in God. Lucan has chosen his path, and the Lord has passed judgement on him. Lucan has condemned himself. At the moment he is lost. But you can save him.'

It was Bedivere who delivered the first blow.

'Sorry,' he whispered under his breath. 'Sorry, Lucan.' Bedivere had been homeless before Art took him in, he'd had a crack habit and had done horrific things to pay for his next hit. But Art had welcomed him with open arms, had helped him come off the drugs. Bedivere needed a home, there was no way he was going back on the streets. He would do what needed to be done, but he wouldn't enjoy it. His friends took up his lead.

Morgana soon followed suit, her strikes were rhythmic, methodical. She put all of her impressive weight behind her attack on Lucan's abdomen, she knew how – she'd done this sort of thing many times before – and soon he crumpled towards the floor. He was not trying to defend himself at all. But he had shut his eyes.

Soon the children joined in, delivering uncontrolled kicks at the body on the floor, girls and boys alike. One or two women gave some slaps, but most stood back and stared, some with tears in their eyes, one or two clenching their fists as though that would allay the unbearable sight in front of them somehow.

King Arthur stayed on the podium, his hands held high in a

worshipful praise to God Almighty. His breathing was slow now, he felt calm. Rejuvenated.

'New Avalon is being cleansed,' he cried. 'And we shall all be saved.'

27

Sister Veronica stared up at the ceiling of her bedroom. Sounds of breakfast being made were going on downstairs and smells of frying bacon and toasting bread had started to waft up to the room. Melissa was taking a shower, and she was angry at herself for being hungry, for wanting her friend to hurry up so they could go down and eat. How dare she still have needs like that when Hope still hadn't been found? How much more selfish and self-absorbed was she going to get, heaven preserve her?

The previous day had been one of the hardest in her life, and she'd lived through some trying times. Beside herself with worry that Celeste had snatched the baby and cremated both herself and Hope in the fire, after all, who knows what strange views she has after being brought up in a cult – Sister Veronica had said to Melissa – she had spent the best part of the day haranguing police officers and anyone else on the high street who looked official and important. How many bodies were found? she'd asked. One, she was told, repeatedly. Are you sure? she'd persisted. Perhaps babies' bones didn't survive fires? Good gracious, she couldn't believe she was having to contemplate such a thing. Only one body was found, she was told yet again. Was it Celeste? she'd asked. The girl who read tarot cards in Goddess World? They couldn't give her any more information, they said. All lines of enquiry were being followed. Was it arson? she demanded. The fire, was it deliberate? Yes, she was told. It was arson. Which is why they were treating the area as a crime scene. That's all we can tell you, they said, motioning for her to move along. She and Melissa had returned to the guest house just after nine in the evening, and as soon as Sister Veronica had lain her head on her pillow deep sleep had come, knocking her into a blank unconsciousness for the whole night.

Good Lord, did Celeste really have it in her to snatch a baby? Sister Veronica had asked herself this at least a hundred times over the last twenty-four hours. Could she really have done it? Sneaked up and quietly taken the sleeping Hope from the pram while she and Melissa had been engrossed in conversation, drinking dashed champagne? She shifted, trying to get comfortable, the gloomy, grey light in the room reflecting both the weather outside and her thoughts. After all, it wasn't just any baby, it was Celeste's niece. The way she'd stared at Hope, the intensity of it, was now etched in her mind. She'd had a motive to take her; she clearly didn't think much of her sister Mona, the way she'd smirked while she talked about her, perhaps she'd wanted to hurt her in some way and seen taking the baby as an opportunity to do this. Or perhaps she wanted to bring the baby up in her ways at the cult, indoctrinating her with some strange Arthurian ways of thinking. But that would be too obvious, surely? If she ever took the baby there the police would find her straight away. And Lucan had said Celeste had vanished, had never returned to New Avalon the night of the fire.

Hope hadn't wanted to be held by Celeste, she hadn't seemed at all comfortable when the girl had held her. Sister Veronica had made light of it at the time, of course, she hadn't wanted the girl's feelings to be hurt. But it had struck her as unusual; Hope was usually happy to be passed round the nuns and parishioners, sociably enjoying all the cuddles she could get and usually charming any newcomers with a toothy grin. She'd never seen her so instantly ill at ease with a person. Mind you, perhaps Sister Irene would have got the same reaction if she'd ever picked Hope up and cuddled her, which, of course, she never had, perish the thought.

The ringing phone, stationed on her bedside table, got her attention.

'Hello?' she said.

'Sister,' the now familiar voice spoke. 'It's Detective Inspector Harding. Listen–'

'Have you found her?' Sister Veronica's words came out fast, rapid fire.

'No, not yet. I'm sorry,' DI Harding's gruff voice said. 'But I do have some news for you. Dental records have confirmed who it was that died in the fire.'

'Celeste?' Sister Veronica said immediately.

'No,' DI Harding said with a sigh. 'I'm afraid it was the girl you've been looking for; Mona. Mona Adkins.'

Sister Veronica's mouth fell open.

'It can't be.'

'It is. I'm sorry to break this to you, I know it must be a shock,' DI Harding said. 'I wanted to tell you now in case the press pick up on it. I saw a few journalists sniffing around when I was on the high street earlier today. They must have an inkling there's a good story for them somewhere in the rubble and ruin. They'll be all over this like parasites when the news breaks.'

Sister Veronica's heart ached. She could hardly talk. The poor girl they'd spent so long looking for. She was starting to feel like she knew Mona, almost as though she was a friend, which was strange because she'd never actually met the girl in real life. The poor creature had certainly been through her fair share of hardships, and Sister Veronica had been harbouring a secret fantasy that she could find Mona and successfully reunite her with her baby, Hope. She was going to offer to help her, maybe suggest a cleaning job at the convent – Mother Superior wouldn't have minded, she was sure – it would have helped get her off the streets. But death was so final. Mona's life on earth had come to an end in a horrific way. And poor little Hope was now motherless.

'Are they certain there was only one body found in the wreckage?' Her voice barely made any sound at all. But she had to ask again, to make absolutely sure.

'Yes, Sister, positive.' DI Harding's tone was reassuring. 'Just Mona. No one else. Definitely no baby.'

A small spark of optimism presented itself in her mind.

'Then Hope may still be alive,' she said, strength coming back into her voice. 'That's what it seems like, doesn't it, Inspector?'

'Yes, absolutely,' DI Harding said. 'Try not to worry too much. I know that's easy for me to say, but like I said, in these sorts of cases the baby or child is usually found safe and well.'

'Oh dear me, poor, tragic Mona,' Sister Veronica said. 'She didn't deserve this.'

'No, she didn't,' DI Harding said. 'From what the emergency services found, it looks like it was murder. Someone intended to kill her. I'm afraid I'm not allowed to give you any other details at the moment. But as you – and the rest of Glastonbury Town – seem to know, the fire was started intentionally at many sites round the house, and is being treated as a serious arson attack.'

Sister Veronica thanked her for her help, and they said their goodbyes, with DI Harding requesting that Sister Veronica phone her immediately if she saw Celeste anywhere, as she was a person of interest they most definitely wanted to talk to.

Melissa wandered back into the room wearing a dressing gown, her wet hair piled up in a towel. An intoxicating freshness – a mixture of soap and shampoo – floated into the room with her. A strange reminder that normal life had to go on somehow amid turmoil.

'Oh, Melissa, there you are.' Sister Veronica heaved herself into a sitting position. 'Sit down, dear, please. DI Harding's just phoned. There's something I have to tell you.'

Melissa took one look at her friend's face and sat down sharply on the bed.

'What is it, Sister?' she said. 'Tell me what's happened?'

28

Celeste lay next to the fretting Hope on the bed of her newly rented static caravan, her long golden hair splayed out over the pillow. She was feeling tired but victorious. It had been a long night, and she'd had to stay awake for most of it, keeping the baby warm in a large blanket she'd taken from the shop for that very purpose. It was a strange but wonderful experience looking after an infant, she'd never done it before, not like this. Of course, there were children at the commune, but their mothers had nursed them as babies. And she'd never felt any real connection with any of them, had always been more interested in her own life. But this was different.

Now miles away from New Avalon in a large camping and caravan park just outside Barnstaple, Devon, she was wondering how her depraved and wicked sister had managed to produce something so beautiful and perfect. A tiny human being who was fresh and unspoiled, with a mind like a blank slate, ripe for learning. Ripe for being brought up the *correct* way. And Hope belonged to *her* now. She'd have to change the baby's name, of course, get her some new clothes and all the other things she'd need. She'd managed to pick up some nappies, bottles and formula from an all-night supermarket on the way, so they had what they needed for now. It had been exciting to choose them, she'd never had to do that before, browse along the baby aisle where all the tired mothers usually stood. Hope had cried the entire time they were in the shop, which had been challenging. But she'd been hungry, had drunk two bottles in a row. It wouldn't be long before they moved away from Barnstaple to somewhere more suitable, where they could really start living together properly as mother and child. She just needed a bit of time to think about their next move, it was important that she get it right.

Getting to Barnstaple hadn't been a problem. She'd been hoarding a healthy stash of money at Goddess World for some time. Much as she loved Art and New Avalon she'd never wanted to be trapped there if something bad had happened, had wanted a way out if the time came. Everything that had happened with Mona and Lance had given her that idea; her sense of security had been jeopardised again like it had when her mother died, and she'd known she had to take steps to protect herself. She had to look after number one. And when that interfering old nun and her tall trashy sidekick had walked in, asking all their questions and announcing that the baby was her niece, she had known that the time had indeed come for action.

She wasn't sure why the name Barnstaple had grabbed her attention, there was something weirdly familiar about it although she'd never been there before. It was probably a sign, she'd decided. Art had always taught her to look out for signs and symbols from God. A few night buses, a quick negotiation with the teenage boy at reception in the early morning, and she was in, ready to start the next fantastic phase of her life. She had no ties in Devon, there was no reason why anyone would look for her there, she was sure of it.

Inviting Mona to meet up hadn't been her idea; that little gem had come from the one person who turned out to hate her sister even more than she did. She'd been surprised about that, but the help had been much appreciated. Her collaborator had tracked Mona down easily, and Celeste had managed to glean more details about her new whereabouts after getting Lucan out of his mind on drink one night. He'd eventually told her that he'd gone to see Mona, and that he still loved her, how he felt guilty that he couldn't protect her from Art. He'd even spilled out her address. It had taken quite a bit of encouragement, but Celeste – after all – was a master at that. Trained by the king himself from a young age. She was pretty sure Lucan had no memory of this; he'd passed out not long after telling her the information, and had never shown any signs that he recalled anything.

What right did Mona have to complain about their king so publicly at that meeting? Celeste's face twisted into a vicious scowl as she remembered the awfulness, the embarrassment, her beauty immediately vanishing. Art had slept with her – Celeste – too, starting when she was still a child. But it was a compliment; the great King Arthur choosing them as his loved ones. It meant they were special, cared for. He'd explained this to them individually, many times. What part of that did her sister fail to understand? Why did she always have to be so difficult?

Seeing the havoc wreaked on her leader by her sister; how many of the weaker followers had chosen to leave after saying unkind things to him, how his usually happy face had become lined and strained, how he'd become much sadder and more depressed than before. It had hurt her heart. How dare her sister break their community life apart? How dare she destroy the big family she loved so much? Celeste's father was long gone and her mother dead, but the New Knights at the commune were her new, better family, and Mona had ruined it, like she ruined everything. A memory flashed into her brain of a something that had happened when they were children. After their mother had died – which was a blessing – Art had told the two little girls, 'Now you can live freely without her sin spoiling you.' Celeste had been desperate to please her king. She did anything he asked, always smiling, always helpful. There had been a day when Art had told the two of them to tidy the Great Hall in preparation for their meeting that night. Celeste took his command very seriously, spending a long time arranging the cushions and sweeping the floor. But Mona had spoiled everything by doing cartwheels across the freshly swept surface, sending the cushions flying everywhere. 'Stop,' Celeste had begged. 'Art will be cross if he comes back.' But Mona had said, 'I don't care. Cartwheeling is more fun than stupid tidying. You're such a goody two shoes, Celeste.' Art had walked in at that moment, the look of disappointment on his face was even worse than anger would have been. He'd made sure both girls had gone to bed hungry that night, and Celeste had hated Mona for days after, not understanding why she'd so wilfully gone against their leader's words, and why she didn't care about getting them into trouble. She'd never been able to see that life would be so much easier, much more enjoyable, if she just settled down and conformed to the king's wishes.

Things had never been the same after she and Lance left. Art was rougher, less caring with Celeste, and much more paranoid. There had been nights when he'd shouted at her until she was hysterical, shaking and crying as he ranted and raved around the room. He'd accused her of complicity in Mona's actions, saying she knew her sister was planning to humiliate him in front of everyone, slapping Celeste and calling her a liar when she tried to defend herself. And all this because of little, rebellious, selfish Mona.

Celeste believed absolutely in Art's teachings, and in the importance of cleansing the Devil out of someone when they fell off the path to salvation. Capturing Mona and purging her of her heinous, un-Godly thoughts and ways had actually helped her sister. It was for her own good. Yes, it had felt good to make her suffer, but now she actually had a chance of getting to heaven. Of course Mona had never realised that, had only looked at her with hurt and hate when Celeste had gone up to the boiler cupboard. She'd taken advantage of the fact that she was the sole person whoever went up the stairs, she was in charge of sorting out stock – the manager of the shop had said on the telephone from his ex-pat home in Spain – and lazy old Liz who worked there a few days a week would never bother going up, it was all she could do to drag herself to work some days. There was no toilet up there, nothing for Liz to ever look at. Yes, it had been a gamble, but she'd made sure Mona stayed quiet. And it had paid off.

Learning that Mona had a baby daughter had been a genuine surprise. Lucan never said anything about that; but then she couldn't have been born when he'd gone to see her sister. Maybe he was the father? Or was it silly little Lance, the boy who'd always idolised Mona but loved cocaine just a little bit more? It was more likely to be one of Mona's dirty punters, more likely that the stupid whore probably didn't even know who the father was.

Well, it didn't matter now, because Hope was safe with her Auntie Celeste. Now, she wouldn't fall to the evil sins of the world, she would be brought up with honour, loyalty and integrity, just how Art would want. And she had plans to do with that too; at some point she would get word to Art, tell him what she'd done, how she was now Mona's baby's mother. He would understand, he always wanted infants to be born at New Avalon so he could save their souls from birth. She knew he'd be furious that she'd disappeared. Celeste giggled as she imagined him going mad, making everyone look for her. But she'd bring him round, she was good at that. Knew all the tricks. She could visualise it now; her and Art setting up home somewhere away from Somerset for a while, passing off Hope as their own, and living purely and simply within their own beliefs. She knew he had enough money to support them for a long while, he'd been hoarding it for years. Sometime later, maybe they could go back to New Avalon, revamp it, and recruit some new, loyal followers. And she would be queen there; she'd have almost as much power as Art. Celeste knew she was beautiful; she loved using this to her full advantage, being able to bewitch men, women and children alike and have them fully under her spell before they knew what was happening. This is how she would rule New Avalon one day, she thought, everyone would love and revere her. Oh, and the clothes she would wear; she could picture them now. So sumptuous and feminine, all the women at the commune would be sick with envy when they looked at her.

The fire at Goddess World had been a shock. She knew it meant that Mona was dead, and she was surprised at how little she cared about that. Seeing her sister suffer in that tiny cupboard had made Celeste content, watching Mona's strength and fight go out of her meant that the cleansing was working. She hadn't thought of killing her, but her accomplice – who never actually went to see Mona in her prison, but who supplied Celeste with increasingly inventive tools to purify her with – obviously had. She wasn't sure of the reason, maybe to cover their tracks? She didn't really care, it wasn't her problem anymore.

Celeste rolled over and hugged Hope, who kicked her legs and let out a whimper. One more cuddle before it was time for a bottle of warm milk. She was so lucky to have found her beautiful baby. She deserved her. And she was *never* going to let her go.

29

'How much does the history of a place influence its residents' characters, I wonder?' Sister Veronica mused, as she read a display pamphlet on the pub's dining table. Feeling decidedly more positive since finding out Hope may well be healthy and alive somewhere, she and Melissa had decided to lunch at what claimed to be Glastonbury's oldest pub, The Bell Inn, in order to stoke up their energy and discuss their next move. Dodging the furious phone messages left for her at the guest house by Mother Superior, Sister Veronica wanted space to think. She would face the wrath of Sister Julia when the time came, and take whatever punishment was doled out to her with humility. She did – in fact – feel she deserved harsh retribution for allowing Hope to be taken, not that that would make anything right, but it would go some way to dealing with the sick culpability she felt inside. But right now, she needed to be in Glastonbury, not summoned back to Soho Square. Melissa's phone was on the table in front of her, and she glanced frequently at it, urging DI Harding to ring with good news.

'What do you mean, Sister?' Melissa said shortly, sitting down and pushing a glass of pale-green liquid towards her friend, an aroma of cigarette smoke arriving with her. She knew she sounded tetchy, but she still felt irritated by the rude barman's attitude. A beautiful old pub it might be, but the rustic interior with its stained-glass windows and old oak tables was much less appealing when you've just arrived at the bar and had your head bitten off while attempting to order a drink.

'What?' the barman had snapped, as she'd grinned around hopefully from the counter, his pinched face peering through a doorway behind the bar.

'Er, two apple juices, please,' Melissa had said politely.

'Stand away from the bar,' he'd squeaked. 'Don't lean on it. Honestly, can you not see how old the wood is in here? People are wearing a groove in the bar front by lazing around on it. Go on, get off.' He'd flapped his hands, as though shooing away a seagull. 'This building dates from 1416, you know.'

Itching to give him a few choice words of her own, Melissa turned to find Sister Veronica cosily ensconced on a corner bench, looking calmer and more at peace than she had done for days. She sighed. She'd been hoping to retort with a dramatic exit, but she wouldn't disturb her friend, not now.

Instead, she'd taken several dramatic paces backwards, bumping into the woman behind her.

'Two apple juices, please,' Melissa had called loudly to the scowling man. 'And the lunch menu.'

Unaware of her friend's recent hospitality trials – she'd hardly noticed her arrive back at the table – Sister Veronica looked up, surprised.

'Er, well I was just thinking that the account of Glastonbury's history written here is actually rather interesting,' she said. 'It describes how the site has long been a place of duality and change – that it's a place where for centuries, old has co-existed with new, and traditional with alternative, although to be honest you don't have to be a mastermind to work that out, you just have to walk down the high street with your eyes open. To start with, it says there's the legend that King Arthur – who apparently defended Britain against Saxon invaders – is buried here. Very intriguing, I've always found folklore fascinating, there's always a bit of truth to it, in my experience.'

Melissa relaxed, her irritation evaporating as she watched her friend talk.

'You're definitely in the right place to learn about folk tales and legends,' she said. 'This place is brimming with them.'

'It goes on to say that the site of Glastonbury became one of the first places in Britain where Britons and Saxons intermixed and learned to live in harmony,' Sister Veronica went on, pointing to a section of the brochure. 'With Christianity replacing Druidism. Then it talks about the Abbey and the destruction of it in the reformation, and so on. It's just remarkable how Glastonbury Town still has that quality today, of being home to contrasting different spiritual practices, beliefs and residents. Perhaps it's a silly thought to have, but I was wondering if the historical energy of a place can influence its residents in the present day, do you see what I mean? Almost as though there's an acceptability for "being different" here, that's coded into the landscape and flows up through people.'

Melissa thought for a minute.

'Maybe the locals have handed that kind of thing down through the ages through their behaviour,' she said. 'And because the public gets to hear of their ways through the media, it attracts people like Lucan who need a place to express themselves outside mainstream thinking. Blimey, Sister, I wasn't expecting to have to use my brain so much before lunch.'

Sister Veronica nodded, taking a sip of apple juice.

'Perhaps you're right,' she said. 'Learned behaviour and press coverage. I'm sure that's part of it. But the thing is, the media wasn't around two thousand years ago, yet it still happened then.

Duality and different beliefs, I mean. But you're right about Lucan and New Avalon. Glastonbury is just the right place to set up a cult, no one would think anything of it, because so many other beliefs are tolerated here. But that's the dangerous thing, you see. No one has questioned what's been going on in the commune, other than when Mona spoke out. And even then, news of her abuse didn't seem to spread to the authorities, it was contained in the compound. The sad thing is, they have the opposite of freedom of thought in New Avalon, Art's followers are tied in to rigid thought structures by his dictatorship. I imagine most of them joined believing it to be a place of mental freedom, then they ended up getting the opposite. I wonder if Celeste fully bought into Art's ways of thinking?'

'She seemed loyal to him,' Melissa said, playing with her glass. 'She and Mona were raised there, so if that's all they knew it must have been hard to think outside their brainwashing, especially when the fear of God was put into them. Literally.'

'Yes.' Sister Veronica's expression sagged. 'But poor Mona managed it. And look what happened to her.'

'I wonder where Celeste's gone.' Melissa sighed. 'I do think it's her who took Hope, Sister, and who started the fire that killed Mona. I know we are supposed to keep open minds and all that, and perhaps it was a random kidnap, but I feel in my bones it was Celeste.'

'Yes,' Sister Veronica said quietly. 'I have a feeling you're right, Melissa. And if Celeste was holding Mona captive and set the fires intentionally, then she is a very wicked person indeed. But I have a feeling she won't harm Hope; the way she was looking at her was so intense, like she'd just discovered the Holy Grail. I *do* hope that whoever took the baby is looking after her well. I can't bear to think of Hope being uncared for. And to think, we were working so hard on her bedtime routine, and now all of that has been ruined.'

As she spoke, the flickering of a small television screen above the fireplace caught her attention. The words '*Breaking News*' were flashing across the screen in big red letters.

'Look.' She motioned to Melissa, who leaned forward, craning to hear the news anchor's words.

'A man has been arrested outside the Houses of Parliament in connection with the attempted murder of the Secretary of State for Digital Culture, Media and Sport,' the woman was saying seriously into the camera. 'MP Pranjal Shastri was on his way to a meeting at the House of Lords when Mr Gareth Pendragon, having violated security procedures, lunged at Mr Shastri, stabbing him through the left shoulder. Heroic passers-by intervened and pulled Mr Pendragon away, holding him down until police arrived and took him into custody. Mr Shastri was taken to hospital, where doctors say he is said to be in a serious but stable condition. A handwritten poster was left at the scene by Mr Pendragon, that alleges loyalty to a group named New Avalon. An investigation has begun into the incident, and police say they can give no more information at this time.'

Sister Veronica turned to Melissa, whose mouth was wide open.

'Can I borrow your phone, please?' She spoke with urgency. 'I need to phone DI Harding. I've had an idea.'

30

'Now New Avalon really is free from sin.' Art spoke quietly as he watched a television report about his son, Gareth, being arrested. Grainy CCTV footage showed a skinny, tall man with lank hair being wrestled to the ground by armed police. 'Stupid, stupid, silly boy.' He folded his fingers together. So much had happened over the last few days, so much intense unfairness, that Art found he simply didn't care about Gareth being detained. In fact, the news about him had transported him from the fury he'd felt about the still absent Celeste to a place of absolute inner calm. Because he finally understood what God wanted him to do.

He'd make no effort to contact the police to see how his son was, he'd just ignore the situation and hope that Gareth had enough sense not to give the police his home telephone number and address. What exactly had the boy been trying to achieve? Yes, all right, so he'd told Gareth to make him – Art – proud. To do something that mattered, something big. But he hadn't meant to stab an MP for God's sake. He'd been hoping that his words would give Gareth the push he needed to blossom into a strong knight; make him grow up a bit, become the leader he needed to hand New Avalon on to when the time came. Lobby MPs in writing – sure. Art had been doing that for years, using a remote postal box address in Birmingham for the return replies – not that many came. He'd wanted Gareth to become more manly, maybe have a child with one of the young ladies at New Avalon, not that there were many left now. A grandchild he could mould into a better heir than his sons turned out to be. He wanted Gareth to become a good example to the rest of the group, instead of wafting around like a lost soul. But that would never happen now. Art was surprised at how easy it was to let Gareth go, now that he'd proved what a weak disappointment he was.

An idea, that had been at the back of his mind for years as a possible escape route if things got bad, had exploded into fruition since he'd first heard about what Gareth had done. God was talking through him again, telling King Arthur the way forward. It was drastic, but he was quite sure it was the only way. And anyway, he'd always known the end would come at some point. He just hadn't known it would be so soon. It was so hard to maintain a utopia in a corrupt world.

He'd done his best to rid New Avalon of the sinners, betrayers and traitors; he'd purified his followers the best that he could, preparing them for salvation. It had felt wonderful cleansing Lucan of sin. It had refreshed their souls. The man would probably die where he now lay in his hut, Art mused. He seemed close to it now. But that was okay. God was calling them all home now, he'd sent several signs. God didn't want Art to have to suffer the indignity of a police investigation – which would surely happen after what his son had done. God didn't want Art to have to see his beautiful commune and its people ripped apart and analysed on national TV; scorned, ridiculed and misunderstood – turned into the very thing Art hated most; vacuous money-making entertainment for people who couldn't think for themselves, which was the majority of the British. Nothing but mindless sheep. He would have to act fast though. His plan would have to be implemented very soon.

And Celeste was gone. Of course, Art had heard about the missing baby, and about the two nosy cows tramping round Glastonbury looking for the dirty bitch, Mona. Of course he'd heard that a body was found in the fire, and that it was Mona's. Good, he'd thought when he'd heard. She deserved it. One less problem to worry about. 'See – my prophecy came true,' he'd told his followers. 'Mona is burning in hell, she was burning before she even died.'

Now Gareth was gone too, dead to him. He suspected his son had been trying to impress him through rash actions, trying to live up to his words, but what a stupid way to go about it. And Lance was dead. These were all signs from God, Art knew, that were showing him his time on earth had come to an end, calling him home to eternal salvation. King Arthur's work was finished.

He'd been expecting a call from the police at any moment, but it hadn't come. Bedivere had taken down the New Avalon webpage as soon as the news about Gareth broke, but it wouldn't take the police long to come knocking at his door. He knew the Avon and Somerset police force were already aware of him, the way they stared when they saw him in town. Distrustful. Suspicious. He could put them off for a while, of course, when they did come, present New Avalon as the peace-loving hippy commune it was, explain that poor Gareth was mentally ill, that they'd had no idea he was going to do such a terrible thing, that he needed to be locked away for his own safety so he couldn't hurt anyone else, poor soul.

Art glanced over at Morgana, who was staring at the television in his study. It was just those two in there, he'd sent everyone else out to hunt for Celeste again. Her giant breasts were heaving up and down as she breathed. He'd suspected for a while that she wanted more from their friendship, but large women – particularly older ones – had never turned him on. Art liked his conquests to be young and pert. And he liked a challenge, a girl with a bit of fire. If someone offered themselves on a plate to him it was just too easy. He'd never tell Morgana that directly, though, just keep her interested enough to be useful. Her intelligence impressed him, her research skills were second to none; he could do with a few more people with brains around here. So he gave her the odd wink, the odd squeeze. It seemed to make her happy. Her face was expressionless as she watched Gareth being escorted away for the ninth time. They'd watched the news on replay many times, as though watching it on repeat would somehow make the awfulness of it – the exposure of their home – go away.

Art thought hard. Would it be wise to take Morgana into his confidence? Explain his plan to her? He'd have to, he decided. He'd need help implementing it, didn't think he could do it on his own. All the New Knights loved Auntie Morgs, they'd do what she asked, even if they had doubts about what their king was saying.

'Morgana,' he said, his voice rich and calm. 'God has spoken to me this afternoon. He's passed on a wonderful next course of action to me, for the New Knights and myself. And we all thoroughly deserve to reap the rewards it will bring.'

Morgana paused the television and leaned forward, a smile breaking out on her face. Since Celeste had gone, she'd been spending more time with Art than ever, and it was wonderful. He'd been increasingly taking her into his confidence, relaxing into trusting her fully, sharing the all-consuming anger and grief he was suffering from inside. She'd been worried about him after the news about Lance, but today he seemed more peaceful, all the anger had stopped, thank goodness, and a strange serenity had taken him over.

'Yes?' she said. 'What is it? I'm all ears.' She gazed at him. *Hang on*, she thought, *Art's eyes looked strange today.* A small, niggling feeling kicked into life at the bottom of her stomach. They were unusually bright and staring, like flashlights that wouldn't turn off. She'd never seen them like that before. She squashed the feeling down, ignoring it. He was just sad about Lance, that was all, which was completely understandable. Going through different phases of grief, it was only natural. And, of course, he was puzzled about Gareth's actions, worried about the impact they may have on their wonderful home life. But he'd get over it eventually, with her unending love and support. Everything was going to be okay.

'God has told me that Armageddon is coming, Morgana.' Art leaned forward. It was so important that he imparted this news in the right way; he'd found that much of the effectiveness of leadership was in his delivery, how he said things. 'Destruction and disaster are nigh; in fact, they are already in process. Just look around at the state of the world and you will see this. The time is right for us to leave earth now. The Almighty is calling King Arthur and his merry band of knights home. As his ambassador here on earth he's chosen me to spread this message among you. And he wants *you* to help lead his chosen people out of a corrupt world, Morgana. God loves and trusts you.' Art's eyes widened. He allowed a smile to form on his lips. 'The good energy is gone from this place now, God has explained everything to me today. The representatives of the lower powers here on earth – like the police – have begun meddling with our destiny, as the Lord, and even I, always knew they would. What the Almighty has asked us to do, what I am about to inform you, will be the ultimate test of commitment, loyalty, and integrity for our knights. And I know you will stand strong beside me, Morgana, and help me lead and guide everyone through this. The truth is that our mission here on earth is coming to a close, and we are returning to God our Saviour for eternal life.'

Morgana's eyes registered the horror that the niggling feeling had quickly morphed into.

'What are you saying, Art?' Her voice cracked. No, he couldn't mean what she thought he was trying to say. After all her hard work getting to this point. After the nights she'd spent fantasising about the perfect life they were going to have together. She'd planned everything so carefully, had executed it with admirable precision, and had been slotting into her new role as Art's closest companion quite comfortably. Surely he couldn't mean...

'Morgana, don't be scared.' Art touched her hand, and despite her growing dismay a thrill shot down her spine. 'It is time to leave our physical bodies and gain our eternal spiritual ones with the Lord, for whom we will always be knights, his right-hand men. If we stay on earth any longer, our souls will be killed by external worldly dark forces, can you not see? That process is already beginning, and we need to remove ourselves from it. To save our true selves we must aid the transformation from persecuted physical beings to eternal saved knights.'

'No, Art,' Morgana whispered, tears springing to her eyes. 'I think you might have misheard what God was trying to say to you.' *No*, she repeated again to herself, *this can't be happening. Not after I'd just made everything so perfect. We are supposed to spend the rest of our lives ON THIS EARTH TOGETHER, Art, why can't you see that?* Of course, she couldn't say the words out loud. Her cherished king wouldn't understand them yet. Her plan had been to give him time to digest his recent tragedies, before slowly but surely encouraging him to rely and depend on her – the most loyal and caring knight of all – until they were one unit, inseparable, tied together forever within the bond of grief, recovery and dependency.

'Of course, you're shocked.' Art smiled, rubbing her hand. 'I was surprised, too, when God told me about it, when He revealed our next and final mission on this physical plane. But it makes perfect sense, Morgana. You'll come to see that soon. And it's a plan we must put into action without delay. I will need your help, and I know that I can count on it, can't I? You've never let me down before.' His saucer eyes stared into hers; encouraging her, willing her to agree.

'But, what about Celeste? We haven't found her yet, we can't leave her behind, surely?' Morgana had changed tack and played her trump card, knowing the girl was his one weakness, his only apparent Achilles heel. She had personally always found the annoyingly beautiful, skinny, self-centred child an irritation, however good she'd been at hiding her feelings, and it was galling to see Art's constant obsession with her. In any case, she'd been intending to tidy up that loose end soon. She'd just had to change direction with her plans a bit, after events had taken an unexpected turn when Celeste didn't return home.

It hadn't been hard to track the girl down, after all, Morgana was excellent at research. Celeste was so like her mother it was unbelievable. Did she really think no one from New Avalon would search the caravan parks after what her infamous parent had done? Morgana could remember the day that Jemima – Mona and Celeste's mother – had been thrown out of the commune by Art. She'd been a lost cause by then, vacant and useless, dependent on drugs rather than on King Arthur. Art had relished the thought of having Jemima's two daughters to himself, of moulding them into perfect knights. The woman had left the compound, taken a bus to a cheap caravan park on the outskirts of Bristol, and shot enough heroin into her arm to kill a horse. When the caravan park manager eventually unlocked the caravan door, after repeated attempts to contact Jemima to ask her to pay her bill, she'd been dead for days.

For Celeste, who'd been born and brought up at New Avalon, her mother's example of how to leave the commune, where to go, was all she knew, the only behavioural model she had to base her own on. She might think she was sassy and strong and had the world at her feet, but in reality she was inexperienced and unworldly. Admittedly, she'd chosen a different area to her mother's, Morgana had been mildly impressed about that, but a few phone calls had located her in less than an hour. Perhaps without knowing it, Celeste had chosen the place where her mother Jemima had been born. She doubted whether she consciously remembered it, she would never have willingly left a trail to herself and the baby, she thought. But something in her had remembered, and it had helped Morgana no end. 'I'm looking for my daughter,' Morgana had said, describing Celeste's hair, her beautiful golden skin and her striking Renaissance clothes. 'She has a baby girl with her, but she's suffering from postnatal depression and I'm so worried. Please, is she at your park?' 'Yes,' the young lad in Barnstaple had said. 'We have a young lady and baby here who match your description.' 'Don't tell her I'm coming,' Morgana had said. 'She's not well, I don't want her to do anything stupid. I'll surprise her, it will be for the best.'

If mentioning Celeste made Art reconsider his crazy plan then she was prepared to talk about the girl all night until her beloved came to his senses. She'd bite down her bile, her anger, and become lovely, motherly Auntie Morgs again, who cared about the girl she'd helped raise. She hadn't always hated her, had seen potential in the child who had been so obedient, so much more compliant than her wild sister. But then Art had got his claws into her and hadn't let go, because Celeste knew how to play him, knew how to use her feminine wiles to always keep him wanting more. And that was no good, it really wasn't.

But as soon as he heard the girl's name, Art withdrew his

hand from Morgana's, his eyes turning dark, his breathing turning faster, shorter.

'She's made her choice,' he said. 'It turns out she's just like her older sister after all.' He sighed. 'And I thought she was so perfect. I thought she was all mine. Morgana, Celeste leaving is one of the reasons God has given us this new mission. He knows that my body needs hers, and I that can't go on without her at my side. Celeste leaving is a sign. God wants to end my pain through this one last challenge, as well as saving all our souls, do you see? I can no longer lead New Avalon if she's not here, I just can't. I never thought she'd go. She was my light and my guide. She could calm me down and she could bring me up. Her and only her. But I see now that her disappearance is symbolic of what needs to happen to us all. It's a sign, can't you see? We all need to disappear, she was showing us this through her actions.' He paused, his brow wrinkling, a deep sigh. 'I know you'll understand as you loved Celeste like a daughter, didn't you?' He didn't look at Morgana while he was talking so couldn't see the venom in her eyes. 'Of course you did, everyone loved Celeste. I never realised how much I did until she chose to go. But she's gone now, made her choice to leave and now she's on the path to hell. And that's broken me, the thought of her suffering forever. But by cleansing ourselves we will be helping her have one more chance at salvation.'

The white-hot rage in Morgana's head was ballooning out of control. She couldn't believe this was really happening. Even in her absence, stupid fucking Celeste was coming between her and Art. For the first time ever, she saw that her king's eyes were wet. Never, in all her years at New Avalon, had she seen Art cry. Not when Mona said those terrible lies, not when Lance died, and not when Gareth left – silly boy that he was. She doubted Art would ever want to see him again. Celeste had got through to Art in a way she – Morgana – seemingly couldn't. She'd captured his heart, and she didn't deserve to, not one bit. And Morgana hated her for it, felt a bitterness and vengeance that was as terrifying as it was all-pervading. And now she was supposed to kill herself to save Celeste's soul? There was no way that was ever going to happen. *You must be joking.* Someone would soon be sacrificed to make New Avalon pure again, she knew, but it certainly wasn't going to be her.

'Let me think about it.' She forced her face into a smile. It was important that Art never suspected how she felt about his protégé or he might guess she knew more than she was saying, torture the truth out of her and go and save the bitch. 'I need to go out for a bit, Art, get some fresh air. What you've said is so overwhelming and amazing, I just need some time to let it sink in.'

He nodded, understanding.

'Don't be too long,' he said. 'I'm going to start getting the medicine ready.' He smiled, his face beatific, radiant. 'God will guide me through the process. He's already told me where to start.'

Morgana left Art's study, grabbed a set of car keys from the rack in the corridor, and marched back to her hut. She quickly changed out of her bodice and skirt, pulling on a T-shirt, jumper and jeans. Her 'external' clothes, as she thought of them. She dragged her special bag out from under her bed, the one no one knew about, made sure everything was in it that should be. As she slammed the door and set off, her face was a contortion of unbridled hatred. That bitch had ruined everything she'd worked so hard to put into place. And now she deserved a little visit from Auntie Morgs.

31

Kay could see the petrol station. It was about two hundred yards away from where she lay, cars driving in and out of it. She was tired, so weak. She'd gone through hunger and out the other side a long time ago. No one had brought her any food for three days and she knew she'd get in trouble if she asked for any. She wasn't supposed to go anywhere near the Food Hall or the Great Hall, most of the residents seemed to have already forgotten she existed. She'd had some stale water before she left, some rainwater that had collected in a broken gutter, but had no bottle to bring any with her for the one and a half mile walk to the garage. It had taken hours to build up the courage to leave, but after what she saw the other night – standing there peeping through the doorway to the Great Hall while her 'friends' had beaten Lucan senseless, blood oozing from his ears, eyes and nose, his arm bending the wrong way – she knew she had no choice. She'd heard the commotion going on, the screams, and she'd had to have a look, the noise was too terrible. She hadn't intervened, knew she'd be killed if she tried, and that would have been no use to Lucan at all. But she'd crept into his hut last night, gone to his bed where the men had deposited him after the attack. He was unconscious, barely alive, his breathing shallow and erratic. She also knew her life would be over if Art or Morgana caught her leaving the compound, but hey, she was probably going to die anyway so it hadn't mattered by then. Lucan had always been kind to her, one of the few that had. The effort of walking with her starved body was hard, she'd had to stop several times and sit down. This time she'd lain on the grassy verge by the road, she didn't even have the energy to sit anymore. She was so close, she just needed to get to a phone, to call help for Lucan. If he didn't get to hospital soon he would die. If he hadn't already. He was her friend, she had to help him. She would close her eyes just for a minute, she thought. If she rested just for a little bit she might get enough energy back to reach the garage.

32

Sister Veronica lowered herself onto the scratchy grass. She was at the top of Glastonbury Tor; a satisfyingly-shaped conical hill that had turned out to be much steeper than it looked. She was ignoring the two large sheep that had come to stand next to her. She wouldn't bother them if they returned the favour, she'd decided, turning her head away to stare at the vista below.

It had been tough when DI Harding had closed down her suggestion about talking to Gareth Pendragon. Had plunged her straight back into despair and darkness, the one thing she felt she could do to help obliterated.

'No, I'm afraid that's impossible, Sister,' she'd said immediately in her matter-of-fact voice. 'Gareth is being held in London by the Met, and neither you nor anyone else – apart from his solicitor – will be allowed to see him at the moment. His charges are very serious. There will come a time when I can interview him and ask him what he knows, we just need to be patient for a little longer.'

Sister Veronica had left Melissa, looking tired and wan, in their guest-house bedroom, chatting to her partner Chris on the landline phone that came with the room. Things had become strained between the two of them, the stress of Hope's disappearance was too much to cope with. They'd started to bicker about the smallest things, getting on each other's nerves, pulling apart instead of together at this appalling time. Melissa's constant smoking was annoying, even though she always went outside to the guest-house garden for a 'fag' as she called them, the smell lingered and their shared bedroom now stank unbearably. Sister Veronica had suddenly needed to get away from her friend, the smelly room, away from everyone and everything around her. Even Glastonbury Town, a quirky place she'd surprised herself by rather liking, was feeling oppressive now. She wanted to be away from the buildings, cars, concrete, broomsticks, incense smells and all the people milling around. And definitely away from the burnt-out building, a scar on the landscape, and a constant reminder of Mona's demise and her poor baby's abduction.

Sister Veronica knew she'd turned snappy and was being downright rude at times, and she knew this wasn't fair on Melissa. But she didn't care, couldn't stop the awfulness she felt inside from coming out in her behaviour. She knew she was already in enormous trouble with Mother Superior, who'd left a message with the guest-house reception saying she was on her way to Somerset, and even more so with the higher-ranked clergy in the diocese, due to the reckless stupidity of her actions. But she didn't care about that. She knew she deserved whatever punishment and humiliation they gave to her. Her heart only ached for the smiley, beautiful Hope; her thoughts constantly dragged to dark ruminations about what could be happening to her. Would whoever took her be keeping her safe? Would they be doing terrible, unspeakable things to her? Would they keep her warm enough? The September nights were becoming increasingly chilly. No one could answer these questions, of course, and it was the helplessness of not knowing that was making her go crazy.

They'd agreed she'd take Melissa's mobile phone with her on her walk, in case anyone needed to urgently contact her. Not that anything fruitful had happened yet, no good news from the police or anyone else had come. She feared it never would. Too much time had passed now, like DI Harding had said – the first twenty-four hours were the most critical, and they were long gone. They may never find Hope now. She'd read too many accounts of child abductions over the years, knew what the end result could be. And that thought was too hard to bear. Melissa hadn't said goodbye when she'd left, hadn't even looked at her, pretending she was too engrossed with her phone call.

Sister Veronica's need to escape had been huge, she'd begun pacing the room, as restless as a hungry tiger, causing Melissa – who preferred to sit quietly and think – to frequently sigh heavily with annoyance. The Tor had seemed like her obvious destination. She'd stared at it enough from the bedroom window, wondering what it was like up there. It had looked a lot lower from the town, she thought now. She'd briefly considered visiting Chalice Well and its surrounding gardens instead, but the hippy girl at reception – the one with dreadlocks and intriguing piercings all over her face – had said the space around Chalice Well was much smaller and all enclosed, and if she wanted to really get away from it all then the Tor was her best bet. The climb had started off all right, but as she neared the summit she'd begun wheezing, had to sit down a few times. The gradient was much sheerer than it looked from ground level. How some people apparently made it up here on a daily basis was beyond her.

There was a real peace to be found up on the Tor, she mused, looking about. It felt isolated, almost otherworldly, even though a few other people were around. There were a group of

Hare Krishna followers dancing near the ancient structure of St Michael's Tower. Some other individuals and couples were walking about, chatting quietly, and a dog ran about gleefully, but it wasn't busy and she'd intentionally chosen a spot as far away from everyone as she could manage.

She had to admit that the tarot card situation had really thrown her. The fact that the Destruction card had been found on Hope, then reappeared in the reading Celeste did for her – although perhaps the girl had fixed it like that with sleight of hand – followed by the actual fire that burnt down Goddess World – well. It was all a bit too much of a coincidence for her liking. She'd never had anything particularly against alternative religions; her philosophy was that if people found something that made them feel good and gave meaning to their lives, then fair enough, no harm done. What she vehemently objected to was the manipulation that could take place with something like tarot cards; a reader could either imbue her customer with confidence for the future or absolute dread, just by flashing a few cards around. There must be a logical solution to the Destruction card, how it seemed to have foretold the actual fire. But the answer to that, the actual explanation, was not clear to her at the moment. Another mystery.

For a while she considered what her next course of action should be. She knew she had to do something, anything, to help find the baby. She couldn't just sit around like a useless lump doing nothing. The best thing to do would be to pay a visit to New Avalon, she decided, speak to this unsavoury-sounding character Art. If he found out she was a nun he might turn against her, if Catholicism offended his own ideals in any way. But that didn't matter, he was hardly going to be delighted to see any outsider descend on his commune, asking questions. But she had to see if he knew anything about Hope. Maybe while she was there she could poke around a bit, talk to some of the residents, see if she could pick up on any clues that someone there might have taken her, or have some knowledge of it. Should she ask Melissa to accompany her there? she wondered. No, probably not. She didn't want to get her friend into any more trouble. She should probably have never even asked her to come to Glastonbury. This was one mission that she would definitely have to undertake alone, and suffer the consequences, whatever they might be.

It was almost like being up on a cloud, she thought, staring down at the patchwork landscape below, where little roads and rivers divided up the fields, houses and gardens. The air was fresh and delicious to breathe in. She felt separate and cut off from the world, and for a moment life seemed a tiny bit calmer. Feeling more at ease now that she had formed her next plan of action, she closed her eyes and let herself drift away.

The phone rang.

She sat up, fumbling to find it in her skirt pocket. Why did it always take so long to find the blasted thing when it was ringing?

'Sister?' It was DI Harding. She sounded unusually animated. 'A baby girl's been found. We think it might be Hope. Can you come and meet me at the police station right away?'

33

'Hello?' A voice was saying. 'Hello? Are you okay? Do you need some help?'

Kay opened her eyes. A young man wearing a luminous-yellow high-vis jacket was staring down at her, a worried expression on his face.

'Phone an ambulance,' was all she could say to him. 'Please.'

'Are you ill?' The man pulled a phone from his pocket, then crouched down to get a better look at her. 'Do you need some water? I can go and get some, I work at the garage just over there.'

Kay breathed deeply, working up the energy to speak again.

'The ambulance is not for me,' she whispered. 'It's for Lucan. He's at New Avalon. Please, he needs one now or he's going to die.' She closed her eyes.

The worried man tapped 999 into his phone, watching as the young lady's eyes closed again.

'Stay with me,' he muttered as the operator answered. 'Come on, love, stay with me.'

34

Art undid the padlock on his allotment gate, breathing in the horticultural scents around him. Then he stopped, allowing himself a moment of pure bliss before he walked on, looking around at the beauty of his carefully planned utopia; the rolling green fields to one side of him, the woodland and orchard on the other, and the neatly divided allotments in front of him. Every knight at New Avalon had a designated patch – even the children – where they were supposed to grow their own wares in addition to the communal ones sewn in the fields. It made dinner time more fun, the chefs for that evening often added herbs and spices to the meals that only they grew. Only Art's patch was off boundaries to everyone else; only he was allowed the privacy and autonomy he kept from his followers. The money his followers gave him from their jobs maintained New Avalon, of course, but none of them would need to work for much longer. Where they were going, God would look after them and they could relax into His care forever.

Always knowing there might come a time when God called King Arthur and his knights home in a hurry, Art had spent years cultivating an impressive crop of Cicuta, otherwise known as Water Hemlock, in his allotment, far away from the fence where prying young fingers could reach. One day, several years before, God had given him a sign to do this by drawing his attention to an article in a newspaper he was reading about the deadly properties of the plant. *'This is your safety net,'* the Lord has said. *'Grow this in your allotment, King Arthur, and all will be well.'* So he had.

Walking into his patch, and grabbing a basket and some thick gloves from his greenhouse, Art began harvesting the tall green plants, throwing bundle on top of bundle until his basket overflowed. The sweet herby smell they omitted as the stalks snapped was not unpleasant, and he breathed it in, taking care to enjoy earthly senses while he still could. Would there be taste and smell functions in his spiritual body in heaven? he wondered. Well, he'd soon find out.

As he slashed at the plants, Art took great care not to let his skin touch the stems, knowing a bad rash could form if it came in to contact with skin. He wanted his actions to remain private, there must be nothing out of the ordinary showing on him; no one must stop him from carrying out his mission. And more pertinently, it only took a small amount of ingestion of Cicuta to bring about death, and he couldn't afford to set off his own transition too early. God had made it clear he wanted *all* the knights to come home, no one was to be left behind. And he intended to make the mixture so strong that there wouldn't be any casualties still alive at the end, no one left behind being criticised and bullied in a hospital for their brave actions. The Externals would never understand the New Knights, but that was because they hadn't chosen to redeem themselves, which was sad in a way.

Art knew death was just a doorway, not an ending. It was going to be a beautiful experience; he imagined himself gliding triumphantly from one life to the next, drifting up a white street towards God. Perhaps there would be knights lining the way, cheering him on as he passed. 'All hail King Arthur', they would cry. And God would beam proudly at him. Congratulate him on his hard work on earth, wonder at the purity of him and his followers, and commend him to heaven for everlasting peace and salvation.

He wondered who to send the video to just before he took his own life later that day, the one he'd just recorded on his phone of himself speaking. Maybe a journalist? he mused. Perhaps a television network? Imagining his words being shown on national TV gave Art a thrill and he broke out in goosebumps all over his body. He'd recorded an exit video for himself and the New Knights; it was explanation to the Externals of why they'd chosen to cross over to heaven now. 'I am Arthur Pendragon, the incarnation of the returned messiah, King Arthur,' he had said into the camera. 'Several years ago I returned to earth to save my people, the chosen ones, the New Knights. I spent many years gathering them together, and we have enjoyed a life of peace and harmony at New Avalon in Somerset. The truest amongst them have proved their loyalty to me, and we have spent some time battling the evils of Britain, showing resistance to the corrupt processes of capitalism, greed and the new religion of the media. But now we have to leave. We don't want to cling to our earthly bodies anymore in this immoral world, we are ready to embrace eternal joy. Our souls will join God and he will praise us for our work. None of the New Knights have been forced to take this step, they were willing and happy to do it. They have chosen God over earthly depravity, and should be commended for that. I came back to this world to offer a doorway to God for his chosen knights, and those loyal to the cause have now proved themselves and are willing to walk through that door now. Today, God has made it clear that he wants us all to come home. So home we have gone.'

Yes, Art thought. That would shock all the Externals in the world, all those sitting complacently at home staring at their TVs, not having any individual thoughts of their own. That would show them who the New Knights are. And more to the point, King Arthur. It would be the only worthwhile media broadcast they would ever see. He – Art – would leave this earth in a cloud of mystery and glory, knowing that the confused Externals remaining behind had chosen their own path to hell. They could have come and joined him at New Avalon any time over the years, they could have been saved, but they'd chosen not to do that. And as such, they would in time reap the consequences of that choice. That was the will and way of God.

35

The intensifying exhilaration was almost too much to bear. Hope had been found, DI Harding had said. Maybe. Possibly. It had to be her, it *had* to be. Sister Veronica felt nauseous as she crashed through the door of the police station, immediately seeing Melissa and DI Harding in front of her. Considering it had taken her so long to walk up Glastonbury Tor, her rapid descent had been close to remarkable, even if it had resulted in several blisters on the soles of her feet. Her flailing arms and legs must have been quite a sight for the grazing sheep, she'd thought at the time, as she bombed through patches of gorse and thistle. Cursing her aging years and generous weight, she'd half-walked, half-jogged down the high street towards the police station, her ribcage now heaving up and down as she attempted unsuccessfully to level her breaths.

'Take a minute, Sister.' DI Harding motioned towards the row of chairs in front of the desk. 'Sit down. The baby that has been found is quite well and safe at West Devon Hospital. We can set off there to see if you can identify her in a minute when you feel well enough.'

'I'm fine,' Sister Veronica rasped, leaning on the counter, her jowly face puce. 'West Devon? Good gracious. Please can we go now, I'd rather get there as soon as possible?'

DI Harding nodded.

'Of course. Just so you know the journey will take us a good couple of hours. Whoever took the baby – if it is her – made some effort to get her out of the area.'

Minutes later, the three of them were in DI Harding's dark car, speeding along undulating tree-lined roads. None of them spoke, they didn't need to. Their shared silence was full of anticipation and nerve-wracking expectation. Melissa, dark circles around her eyes, stared out of the window, chewing a piece of her nicotine gum. There'd been a frostiness in her greeting, Sister Veronica reflected, when she'd hurtled through the police station door, which wasn't surprising really. She knew she'd been a pain, a nightmare to live with these past few days. She'd apologise soon, try and make it up to her friend. Smooth things over, and make everything all right. But now all she could think about was the baby. DI Harding sat upright, her grey eyes on the road, driving them all steadily onwards.

Please let it be Hope. Sister Veronica sent up prayer after prayer to the universe, her maker, the source of all energy and anyone else who happened to be listening, as she watched the trees and houses outside whiz by. *Please let it be her, all safe, well and unharmed. I'll do anything to atone for my stupid carelessness, God, if you just let Hope be the baby at the hospital.*

36

Morgana closed the door of the static caravan quietly. Cleansing someone of their evil was a beautiful thing, and she always felt uplifted afterwards. Seeing Celeste's blood had excited her; it had been the same with Lucan's. It was a joyous moment to see the flesh break and the wickedness pour out. It was spiritual, sacrificial, a practice that had taken place down the ages for millennia.

She'd tied Celeste up first, then taken the baby to the church she'd passed minutes before turning into the caravan park. After all, she wasn't a monster, she didn't have any problems with the infant, even if she was the spawn of Mona. But the child was an innocent, and she would leave her fate up to God. She knew the baby would either be found or looked after, or she would die and cross over to the gates of heaven. She didn't really care which. And anyway, the little girl had started screaming and the last thing Morgana had wanted was attention being brought on the caravan before she'd had a chance to finish her work. She'd left the sobbing child on the church steps, memories of placing her on the convent steps in Soho all those weeks ago flooding back to her. Funny how life repeated itself sometimes. Leaving the Destruction tarot card had been a nod towards Celeste, designed to put the trail on to her if the police became interested in the baby's history. A bit of research had resulted in a link to Sister Catherine, which had been even better. Morgana had always loved riddles, they were so satisfyingly bewildering. Creating a real-life one had been thrilling, and she always enjoyed putting her intelligence to the test.

She'd helped Celeste write the invitation to Mona – after all, the girl was more beautiful than she was bright – appealing to her to come to Glastonbury, saying how much she missed her sister and wanted to mend their bond. They'd both been surprised when Mona had accepted. Taking the baby from the drugged-up Lance's care had been easier than she'd anticipated. He probably didn't even remember her knocking on the door, saying Mona had asked her to bring the baby to her, he'd been so out of it. Knowing what she planned for the triad that took up her beloved king's thoughts – Mona, Celeste and Lance – she'd needed the child firmly out of the way. Lance's drug use had been an added bonus, something even she couldn't have planned on. If he'd been sober, then, well, she'd have had to silence him another way. But as it was, he'd self-medicated himself enough; he'd even forgotten the baby was there, lying silently in her crib, big eyes staring up at the ceiling.

She'd always planned to start a fire at Goddess World, of course, to burn the witch Mona as Art would have wanted. She had made it look like it was all Celeste's work, the tarot card, the fire, the killing of Mona. The original plan was that by the time the police caught up with Celeste to arrest her for the carnage created she would already be dead, leaving Morgana and Art to live in blissful, dependent peace for the rest of their lives. The only thing was, she hadn't reckoned on the two wild cards coming into the mix: Celeste taking the baby and running away, and Art deciding mass suicide was a good way for the knights to now leave the earth.

'You need to be punished,' Morgana had explained to Celeste on her return to the static caravan. 'Do you have any idea how much you've hurt King Arthur by running off? You are a wicked girl. You never stop and think about how you might be hurting other people's feelings, do you?'

Celeste, lying on the floor, bound and gagged, had lain still, staring up at her captor with big fear-filled eyes. It had been wonderful to see her so helpless. Morgana had enjoyed leaning forwards and tightening the thin scarf she'd used to muzzle the girl until she could see the edges cutting into her cheeks.

'What's that?' She'd chuckled, drawing a whip from her bag. 'Speak up, Celeste, I can't hear you. Don't you have anything to say for yourself for once?'

She'd relished the flailing of Celeste, and the purging and the beating; all techniques taught to her over the years by her king. The blood had to flow freely for the person's sins to evaporate, Art always said. If you spare them the pain, then you send them to hell. And what's the point of that?

'Do you know what you've done?' She'd bent down to hiss in the girl's ear as her eyes had rolled back. 'You evil little bitch? You've made Art go mad. He wants to kill us all now, because he's lost *you*. He was meant to be *mine* now. That's really why you need to be punished, you shallow cow. You never deserved him. I've always known that, you scheming little whore. And now, after I've waited for him so patiently, you've managed to ruin it all by going missing before I had a chance to deal with you. Can you understand now why Auntie Morgs is a bit cross, Celeste?' She'd stood up and booted the unconscious girl in the head.

As she drove away from Barnstaple, Morgana's joy and satisfaction became infused with grief. She knew she'd never have a chance with Art now, he was hell-bent on his mass suicide idea. Well, there was no way she was partaking in that. Her chest ached as she absorbed the fact that her months of careful planning had come to nothing. Everything was ruined. Purging Mona, the fire, the little trip to see Lance as his 'mother' the night before he'd died (with a vial of morphine in her handbag, how easy it was to shoot into the cannula when no one was looking), all her efforts were wasted. Getting rid of everyone that consumed Art's attention had been an exhaustive process but she'd done it for them, *both* of them, so they could rule a better, purified New Avalon together. He was supposed to depend on her strength, turn to her in his hour of need. But now all he wanted to do was kill himself.

She'd had to get the annoying triad out of the way, she told herself, because Art was in one way or another obsessed with each of them, Mona, Celeste and Lance, so much so that he never seemed to be able to turn his attention entirely on to Morgana. Mona had to go because Art had always said she needed a fiery punishment, so that's what had happened to her. Even though it had been nearly three years since she'd left New Avalon, Art ruminated loudly about Mona each day, asking God to bring death and punishment on her. But she never seemed truly out of his head; he was preoccupied with her in a dark, morbid way.

She'd had to get rid of Celeste because her king loved the girl too much, and she absolutely got in the way of Morgana taking her rightful place alongside Art. Art's obsession with Celeste actually made her want to be sick at times, it was so all-consuming, so obvious. But he liked Morgana too, she knew he did, what with all the secret winks, hugs, squeezes, and confidential chats. She was more Art's intellectual equal, Celeste hadn't been blessed with many brains. And Lance went because his father spent too much time brooding about getting him back, too much time worrying about him, obsessing about the evil Mona having taken his son away. But there was never closure with Art, he never seemed to move on from this, just went on about it every day. Morgana had known a clean slate was needed, and that was what she'd organised. It was supposed to be a fresh start, they could have both grieved, and then all moved on towards a happy future. Together. And now her plans were in ruins.

She let out an animalistic howl as she sped down the near empty roads.

But she was a fighter, she always had been, had learnt that skill from the moment she was born. She knew she'd survive this, feel better eventually.

Her plan was to keep on driving and not look back.

37

'There she is.' Sister Veronica darted forward and lifted the quiet baby from the nurse's arms, hugging her close. Fat tears rolled down her wrinkled cheeks as she breathed in Hope's powdery smell. 'Hello, Hope. I've missed you so much.'

'Are you sure it's Hope, Sister?' DI Harding said. 'Are you absolutely positive?'

'Yes.' Sister Veronica said, sniffing, as she rolled down Hope's green-and-yellow tights. 'She's wearing the same clothes – the ones Melissa bought for her, and look, there's the birthmark shaped like an island that I told you about. It's definitely her.'

'Fantastic, I'm so pleased for you,' DI Harding said. 'I was confident it was her, but I couldn't say too much before you'd positively identified her.' She gave a quick smile, a warm and genuine gesture. 'The doctor has taken some bloods and they are being matched with the ones taken in London, just for legal reasons, to officially confirm everything. She'll be staying here under police protection until we have the results back.'

'Can I have a cuddle?' Melissa's eyes were also streaming with tears. 'I won't take her from you for long, Sister, I just want to say hello to her again, let her know she's safe now, that we've found her.'

'Of course.' Sister Veronica passed the baby to her friend, forcing herself to, although really feeling that she never wanted to let the baby go again. 'You deserve to, Melissa. You've been the most wonderful companion with all your help and support recently, and I'm afraid I've turned ghastly, rude and moody. I'm so sorry, you didn't deserve to be treated like that.'

'That's okay.' Melissa gave the nun a watery smile, as she gently kissed the top of Hope's head. 'We've both been very stressed. I don't think there is a "right" way to act in that kind of situation.'

A voice came crackling over DI Harding's radio.

'Excuse me,' she said to both of them, before turning and striding towards the door. 'I won't be a minute.'

Sister Veronica stared at the sedate but smiling baby girl in Melissa's arms. She couldn't believe it was her, after all this time. The terrible angst, the sleepless nights, the gut-wrenching worry. Yet here she was in front of her, fresh and healthy, although not as exuberant as usual, but that was to be expected, all things considered. She took in every aspect of the baby, drinking in her smattering of fluffy auburn hair, her chubby pink cheeks, her rosebud mouth. The sense of wonder and relief in her heart grew until she was sure her chest was going to explode. Had she been harmed at all? she wondered. Had she been fed and looked after? A baby could never tell you these things, of course. The most important thing was that at last the nightmare was over.

'Would you like her back, Sister?' Melissa said, turning. 'I don't want to let her go, but I think she wants to come to you.'

Hope was indeed sticking her arms out towards Sister Veronica, and as she carefully took the baby again, her heart did a backflip of joy.

A nurse came bustling into the cubicle.

'All reunited, I see?' she said, grinning.

'Yes, thank God.' Melissa smiled. 'Where was Hope found, do you know?'

'All I've been told is that she was found on the steps of St Peter's Church in Barnstaple,' the nurse said as she popped the tip of a thermometer into Hope's ear. 'We've been monitoring her since she got here and she seems perfectly healthy. Bit quiet, but generally fine. Ah, perfect temperature. I think she's just a bit shocked by everything that's happened to her over the last few days.'

'And who can blame her. Great Saints, so she was left on the steps of a religious place again?' Sister Veronica's voice registered her surprise. 'Surely that has to be by the same person who left her on the convent steps the first time? Or at least a person in cahoots, or someone with knowledge of what happened?'

'I wouldn't be surprised,' Melissa said, stroking Hope's hand. 'I still can't believe she's back. It's a miracle.'

'We can't get over her beautiful blue eyes,' the nurse said, filling in Hope's chart. 'We've all had lots of cuddles with her. She's going to break many hearts when she's older, you know.'

'Yes, she's absolutely precious.' Sister Veronica rocked the baby to and fro. 'An absolute darling.'

'Bless her, she's going to sleep,' Melissa said, sitting down in the chair next to Hope's cot. 'Look, her eyes have gone all droopy.'

'She thoroughly deserves to,' Sister Veronica said. 'She's been on quite an adventure, haven't you, young lady? If only you could tell us with who.'

DI Harding came back into the room, her face serious.

'News has just come in,' she said. 'Two residents from New Avalon have been taken into intensive care at Yeovil Hospital.

They're in a pretty bad way, apparently horrifically abused by followers of the professed King Arthur.' She paused, sighed, and shook her head. 'I've got to go over there now. If any connection comes up between New Avalon and whoever took Hope I'll keep you informed.'

38

DI Harding sipped her water. Strictly speaking, guests weren't allowed to eat or drink in the intensive care unit, but she'd been so parched after her hasty drive to Yeovil a nurse had taken pity on her.

'Don't rush,' she said, as gently as she could. 'Tell me in your own time.'

Lucan could only move his eyeballs without his body hurting. Every other body part had to be kept absolutely still. His jaw felt paralysed and he couldn't speak properly. When he tried his words came out all thick and distorted. The doctors had told him he had internal damage to his liver, one of his lungs was punctured, many of his ribs were broken, his pelvis was cracked and he had three skull fractures. Oh yes, and a broken arm and leg. He was lucky to be alive, they said. But he was desperate to tell the detective what he knew. It would just take time and patience, mainly his.

'Art did it,' he said, his words coming out muffled, almost incoherent.

'Art?'

'Yeah.'

'What did Art do?' DI Harding had known about New Avalon's leader for years, oh yes he'd been on her radar all right. She'd heard things about him, rumours and gossip about abuse, beatings, coercion, but nothing ever concrete enough to investigate and no witnesses prepared to give statements. But now, it seemed, the man had gone too far. Her colleagues at the station were already in the process of organising a search warrant for New Avalon, and she was going to enjoy tearing that place apart as soon as she'd finished this interview.

'He said they had to cleanse New Avalon of my depravity and purify my soul,' Lucan managed. It was hard for him to have to think back, relive those awful moments. DI Harding had to ask him to repeat his sentence several times before she fully understood his words.

'I see,' she said. 'So what did Art's followers do when he said that?'

'They beat me.' Tears began to flow down the sides of Lucan's face. 'They kicked and stamped on me. For a long time. Even the children. And he just kept encouraging them, willing them on, saying that New Avalon was now saved.'

'I'm so sorry to hear that, Lucan,' DI Harding said softly. 'That must have been awful. You didn't deserve that. No one deserves to be treated like that. Especially by people they trust.'

Lucan continued to cry. It hurt him to do so but he couldn't help it.

'Would you be prepared to make a statement about what Art and his followers did to you?' DI Harding asked, when Lucan had become calmer, his silent sobs spaced further apart. 'It seems to me that he needs to face justice for what he has done to you and Kay.'

'How is Kay?' Lucan said. The doctors had told him it had

been Kay who'd called the ambulance to New Avalon, had saved his life before collapsing herself. He knew she was somewhere in the same hospital as him and that made him feel a little bit comforted, to know his saviour was close by.

'She's stable.' DI Harding wondered how much to tell Lucan. She didn't want to upset him more than necessary. 'She's sleeping at the moment.' *Still unconscious*, she thought to herself. So thin, poor girl, that her skin looked blue with veins. No one knew if she would wake up, her body was so undernourished her organs had started to shut down.

'That's good.' Lucan relaxed a bit. He wanted to thank her, when he could. Express how much it meant to have one person care about him amid the betrayal and atrocities of his other former 'friends'. But then they'd only done what their leader had told them to. He'd done awful things to heretics before, many years ago, under Art's instructions. Back when he fervently believed it was the right thing to do. Now he knew how it felt, had had a taste of his own medicine. That was why he hadn't tried to fight back, knew it wasn't worth it, that they'd always beat him down. But also because he felt he deserved it, now he understood how wrong it was to hurt others like he had in the past. All because Art said so. He wondered if the people who had damaged, hit, kicked and stamped on him felt bad about it? Probably not, not yet, they were too fearful of doing something wrong that would lead them to the same fate. Maybe one day they would.

'Would you be prepared to make a statement?' DI Harding repeated, staring into his swollen blue eyes, now tinged red with burst blood vessels.

'Yes.' Lucan tried to nod, then winced, a spasm of pain spiralling through him. 'Yes, I would.'

'That's great news.' DI Harding exhaled. 'Well done, Lucan.

You're being very brave.' Finally one of the cult members was going to speak out against the so-called King Arthur, she thought. And it took this to happen before they did. Near death. But that's the way of it sometimes, you have to hit rock bottom for things to change, before you have the emotional strength to go against someone who has put the fear of God into you. She knew she was going to do everything in her power to get justice for Lucan; if there was one thing she hated most in life it was a bully, someone who made others feel small just so they could feel big and important. It was the height of cowardice, she thought, to treat someone like that, especially to encourage a mob attitude that he couldn't possibly have had a chance of escaping. New Avalon was clearly a dangerous place and it needed to be shut down as soon as possible before things there escalated even further out of control. And she would take great pleasure in seeing that happen.

They chatted for a little longer, with her gently pressing Lucan for as many other details as possible, until his eyelids began to droop.

When she was outside the ward again, DI Harding radioed the station. Finally, she and Art were going to meet. She couldn't wait. After all the years of hearing rumours about the coercion and abuse at New Avalon, she had enough information to press charges against him. The apparent King Arthur. Bully and fraud, more like. Once she got him into prison he wouldn't be coming out again to damage anyone else's life, that was for sure. She'd seen some things during her time in the force, sides of human nature that thankfully most of the general public rarely came into contact with. But she'd never come across a case of such clear hypocrisy, where the leader of a group – who called himself God's spokesman on earth, and who duped his followers into thinking he was a perfect example of morality – turned against one of those same followers with no good reason, and coerced others into beating him sadistically to within an inch of his life. No, that was a new scenario to her, and one she never hoped to come across again. The abuse of Art's trust was off the scale, his actions unforgivable. *Right*, she thought, making her way down the sparse hospital corridor. *Let me at him.*

39

'Morgana,' Celeste whispered to the police officer who accompanied her in the ambulance. 'Morgana did this.'

The staff at Barnstaple Caravan Park, suspicious after news broke about the baby girl being found at the church down the road, and putting it together with Morgana's phone call claiming Celeste was suffering postnatal depression, had gone to check on her. Finding the caravan door unlocked, they'd knocked and entered, only to find Celeste lying in a bloodbath on the floor, her eyes half open. Ten minutes later, Celeste, now conscious and under arrest on suspicion of involvement with her sister's murder, was on her way to West Devon Hospital, with PC Channing as her attendant in addition to the paramedic who was carefully giving her a shot of morphine through a cannula for the unbearable pain.

Why had Morgana done this to her? Celeste couldn't see her face but she suspected she would never look the same after this. There was too much blood coming out of her ears and eyes, her cheekbones felt too mushy, and her nose was no longer the right shape. Her golden hair was falling out in clumps around her shoulders. But the ache in her body and limbs, oh the pain was excruciating, she wanted to die, it would be easier than bearing this. And the baby was gone. *Her* baby. Where was she now? What had Morgana done with her? The police wouldn't tell her anything, just turned vague and evasive when she asked any questions.

Her battered thoughts formed only one bitter question; *why am I under arrest for what happened to Mona? I'm the victim here,* she told herself. *She was the dirty whore who brought shame to King Arthur and New Avalon. Morgana – Auntie Morgs – was like my mother; she hugged me, looked after me, helped me cleanse my sister, was there when I needed her most. What have I done to deserve this kind of treatment from her? Why can't the police see I'm the casualty in all this?* Hot angry tears leaked from Celeste's eyes, mingling with the drying blood. The ambulance trundled on, siren blaring.

'The best thing you can do is co-operate with the police,' PC Channing said, her tone flat and disinterested. 'You'll be looked after in hospital until the doctors are satisfied, but as you know, Miss Adkins, you are under arrest on suspicion of the murder of your sister, and for the kidnapping and imprisonment of your niece.'

'But I didn't murder her.' Celeste wept, shaking. Every movement caused pain to reverberate through her body, as though it were just a bag of bones being shaken in a plastic bag. 'I looked after her. I made Mona pure again. And the baby is part of my family, I'm her closest relative. I deserve to have her with me, can't you see that?'

'Like I have mentioned, Miss Adkins,' PC Channing said. 'You do not need to say anything. But, it may harm your defence if you do not mention something which you later rely on in court. Anything you do say at this stage may be given in evidence.'

But I'm barely alive, Celeste wailed in her head, as self-pity consumed her. *Look at me, I'm so injured, so hurt, that I might die. Why is that police officer being so cruel to me? Why is she not looking after me?* Fresh hot tears plopped down the side of her cheeks.

PC Channing sighed. After nine years in service she'd become immune to the self-absorption of criminals. With the majority of them it was never their fault, they could never take responsibility for what they'd done. It wasn't nice seeing Celeste Adkins in this state, of course it wasn't. But she had strength in her, she'd pull through this, PC Channing was sure. Some of the injuries looked worse than they were. And she knew what had happened to Mona, had seen the wreckage of Goddess World, heard that the poor girl had died a horrible death from smoke inhalation and burns. How scared she must have been, knowing she couldn't get out of that cupboard she was locked in, as the smoke came under the door. She'd been roasted alive. No, she didn't hold any sympathy for Celeste Adkins. She's made her choices, and now – however hurt she was – she'd have to face the consequences.

40

D I Harding approached the main building in the compound with Detective Sergeant Miller. Officers had already secured all the entrances to New Avalon and four firearms officers were accompanying them into the building because Lucan had told her that Art and other residents there were in the possession of multiple weapons. More squad cars were on their way and the plan was to take all the inhabitants of New Avalon into custody once they had the leader safely restrained.

It really was a run-down place, she thought, looking around. Rather different to the website photos that made it look like a new-age haven – she should know, she'd studied them enough times in the past. Two large, circular canvas buildings in the middle of a load of drab-looking sheds, or huts. Perhaps they'd looked quaint and rustic once, but now they just looked sad and tired. It all reminded her of a programme about hunting lodges in the Appalachian Mountains that she'd seen once. All the dwellings were spread out among the trees, lonely and desolate-looking, the paths between them just muddy dirt tracks. Only one hut looked taken care of, like a bit of money had been spent kitting it out. It was three times bigger than all the others, and had curtains and double glazing. No guesses who *that* one belonged to, she thought.

She knocked on the wooden door of the large structure in front of her.

'Police,' she shouted. The officers around her paused, listening.

No answer.

One of the firearms officers lifted his foot and kicked. The door swung open; it hadn't been locked. Two of the officers entered the Great Hall before her, stun guns raised.

It was empty. All that was there was a podium in the centre, and a variety of tired cushions scattered around. The slogans on the wall were interesting, they read like a manifesto. Perhaps that's exactly what they were, she thought. She'd have photos taken of every one of them soon.

The group worked their way in trained formation through the hall, past the dragons and written mantras, to the door at the back.

A chinking, glassy sound came from beyond it.

'Police,' DI Harding shouted again.

An officer pushed the door open and walked through, gun raised.

DI Harding stepped forward and saw a long-haired man standing behind the kitchen table. He was alone in the room and he was licking his lips. Numerous glasses – at least twenty – most containing a dark-green liquid, stood on the surface before him. One of them was empty.

'Art Pendragon?' she said. The man raised his dark eyes to meet hers. He said nothing.

'Are you Arthur Pendragon?' she asked again.

The man reached out and picked up a glass, pouring the

green liquid in it down his throat so fast that drops of it splashed onto his long white tunic, a green river slithering down his chin.

'Stop. Put the glass down,' a firearms officer shouted, walking towards him. 'Raise your hands. Keep them where I can see them. Do it now.'

The long-haired man smiled, wiping his mouth before raising his hands in the air.

'Well hello there,' he said, his voice rich and deep. 'Yes, I'm Arthur Pendragon. I'm so pleased to meet you. Welcome to New Avalon, folks.'

Two officers descended on him from either side, grabbing his raised arms, pulling them down behind his back, cuffing him quickly.

'Arthur Pendragon, or in actual fact, Colin Sacks,' DI Harding walked over and stood before him, 'I'm Detective Inspector Harding and I'm arresting you on suspicion of attempted murder.' The man continued to smile while she read him his rights.

'Only attempted?' he said when she'd finished. 'Oh dear, that's a shame. The thing is, I'm afraid I won't be with you for very much longer, Inspector. You see, God has called me home. I'm going to be leaving the earth very soon.'

'What's he talking about?' DS Miller walked over to the table and stared at the rows of drinks. 'What's in these glasses, Colin?'

But Art just smiled, as the poisonous concoction of Cicuta leaves and vodka took hold of his body.

'Call an ambulance *now*,' DI Harding said, turning, her tone urgent, as more officers entered the room. 'We need him alive. He needs to have his stomach pumped as soon as possible. Take a sample from those drinks and send it to the lab, we need to have it analysed. I think he's just tried to kill himself, probably with some sort of poison.'

'I'm afraid you're a bit late for that.' Art's face was flushed, ecstatic, as he looked at her. 'I've had two already. Won't be long now, I should think.' It was a pity he'd been the only one to drink the mixture, would be the only one crossing over to meet God, but everything that was happening was part of the Almighty's plan and he had to submit to it. Of course, he hadn't had the chance to send the recording of his words to anyone yet, but the police might find it on his phone after he was gone and send it to the press. He hoped they would.

'Is that what you had planned for your followers, then, Colin?' DI Harding said, her voice rising. 'A murder-suicide? What a very caring plan. Do you realise how many families you would have destroyed if you'd been able to get everyone to drink these?'

'I'm afraid you've got it very wrong, Inspector,' Art said. 'The New Knights who live here *are* family. They don't need any others. We are one family. And God has called us all home now, and *you* are the one ruining their lives now, not me. If you stop them from taking this final step to salvation, you will be sending them to hell for eternity.'

'That's a risk I'm willing to take,' DI Harding said, her mouth grim. 'My officers are rounding your knights up now, as we speak. I'll be very interested to hear what they have to say about you and New Avalon.'

'They'll tell you the truth, that it's paradise here.' Art's eyes were dreamy.

'Did Lucan Butler think it was paradise,' DI Harding said, 'while everyone was beating him and stamping on him so hard they crushed his liver?'

'How silly the paramedics were to rescue him.' Art turned his big brown eyes on to her, his stare full of reproach. 'They shouldn't have done that. Now his soul is going to hell too. After all the trouble we took to cleanse it.'

'That's enough for now.' DI Harding turned away, unable to

look at the man any longer. He was clearly as mad as a fruit bat. So far gone it would take an expert psychiatrist to scratch the surface of his insanity. But oh, what damage his delusions had caused. But he'd been sane enough to relish controlling others, she thought, coercing them to commit terrible acts. Perhaps a large part of him wasn't mad at all, just power hungry and psychopathic. She wanted him to survive, wanted to be able to hold him accountable for the terrible harm caused to Lucan and Kay. Wanted to question him about Mona, Celeste and the abduction of Hope. Ask him if Gareth's claims, that his father had first given him the idea to kill an MP, were true. She suspected the secrets he held sprawled far beyond whatever she knew about. Hopefully she'd get some answers from his followers too.

'Is the ambulance on its way?' DS Miller asked, watching some green liquid being carefully bagged up.

'Yes, Sarge,' an officer replied. 'Should be here soon.'

'Good,' DI Harding muttered. After what he'd done, that man didn't deserve to escape justice so easily. His cowardly attempt at suicide proved exactly who and what he was. Destroyer of lives, and too spineless to take his own punishment. Well, not if she had anything to do about it.

41

Sister Veronica was still gazing at the baby girl in her arms, breathing her in. She'd hardly put her down since arriving at West Devon Hospital, had only done it once and that was to change her nappy.

'We think we've discovered something quite extraordinary,' Dr Mundra was saying, a smile on his face. 'You're never going to believe it.'

'What's that?' Sister Veronica said, her tone distracted. She was too busy enjoying her closeness to Hope. It was healing to cuddle her again. To feel her soft baby skin, look into her innocent blue eyes. But there was fear also, a fear that this could somehow happen again, that if Hope had vanished once – so easily – she could be taken by someone else.

DI Harding had phoned Melissa, explained that she'd arrested Art, although he'd poisoned himself and was currently very ill in Yeovil Hospital. She'd also said they'd found Celeste, who was in a sorry state after Morgana's attack, but well enough to admit to snatching Hope. 'Please don't worry anymore,' she'd said. 'The baby is safe now. You can relax, start moving on with your lives.' But that was easy for the detective to say, and it wasn't easy for her to do. How could she *relax*, knowing it was her own lax attitude that had led to Celeste being able to take Hope? There may be two police officers standing outside the ward but *she* needed to be vigilant at all times from now on, no matter where she was or who she was with.

'Well,' Dr Mundra said. 'Sister, we believe that we have found Hope's father.'

Sister Veronica's head snapped towards him, his words having got the full glare of her attention.

'Pardon?' she said. 'You've found Hope's father?'

'Yes,' Dr Mundra said with a chuckle. 'Very unexpected indeed, but it looks like we really have. DI Harding asked us to test and compare the blood samples from Hope with all the New Avalon members currently in Yeovil Hospital. So we did. And DNA matching has confirmed there is more than a 99.999% chance of one of them being her father.'

'Oh no.' Melissa stood up from her chair. 'Is it Art? Or Colin, or whatever his real name is?'

'No.' Dr Mundra smiled. 'It's Lucan Butler.'

Sister Veronica gazed at the baby who was staring up at her. Oh, silly of her. Of course, she could see it now. They both had the same bright blue eyes. And hadn't Lucan said he'd gone to visit Mona last year, and stayed the night? Why hadn't she thought of that possibility herself?

'Well, Heavens above,' she said quietly. Hope gurgled in agreement. 'That's absolutely marvellous. You have a lovely daddy, Hope. Who I'm sure will take fantastic care of you, if he recovers.'

'He's doing well, according to my colleagues at Yeovil,' Dr Mundra said. 'He's been informed he's the father of the baby, and is absolutely thrilled, by all accounts. His happy mood will help his recovery no end. In my experience, if you have a great will to live you are halfway there when it comes to getting over his type of injuries.'

'That news has made me feel quite emotional.' Melissa wiped a tear from her eye. 'Oh, Sister, I don't think I can cry any more, my eyes are actually hurting, so many tears have come out of them over the last few days.'

'Ah, but these are happy tears, my dear.' Sister Veronica shifted Hope into one arm and leaned over to give her friend a hug with the other. 'They will help to soothe the pain. The trauma has ended now, and great things have started to come from this tumultuous time.'

The doctor turned to walk out of the cubicle.

'Thank you, Dr Mundra,' Sister Veronica called after him. 'We needed to hear this happy news. Thank you so much.'

As she enveloped Hope in yet another huge cuddle, wetness glistened at the corners of her own eyes. *So this adventure is over for you now, Hope*, she thought. *And another one – a joyous, fantastic one – is just beginning.* Sending up a prayer to God and the universe to heal Lucan as fast as possible, a pang of grief tugged at her heart. But this time it was a necessary kind of sorrow, and she knew what it meant. Her time with Hope was now drawing to a close. When Lucan was well enough, this little bundle would go and live with him, and Great Saints above she was going to miss her.

On the plus side, she realised, Hope had taught her a much-needed lesson and it had helped her to put her past memories of the tragedy with Jamie Markham and his murder to rest. When the little girl had gone missing, and then reappeared a few days later, it had shown her how important it was to live in the present moment, in the 'now', to just enjoy what was in front of her eyes rather than worrying about past ordeals. *Every second is a chance to start over*, she thought. *Thank you, Hope. You've taught me that, you lovely child, and I'm never going to forget it.* She kissed the top of her head.

Dr Mundra's head popped back round the curtain.

'Sorry, I forgot to tell you something,' he said. 'There's a woman waiting for you downstairs by the reception desk, I think she said her name was Sister Julia Augusta. Says she's your Mother Superior. I'll tell you one thing, I'm glad it's you she wants to see and not me. She looks absolutely furious and has been saying the rosary very loudly for at least ten minutes. The poor girl on reception looks terrified.'

42

SIX MONTHS LATER…

In the end, Sister Veronica had chosen a picture book about Noah's Ark to bring Hope as a gift. It had taken her a while to decide as she perused the bookshop's shelves, wanting to find just the right story, something meaningful. After all, the child would be nearly one now, much more observant and able. And one day she would be old enough to understand at least part of what had happened to her and her mother. If that information was hard for her to process, it was important she understood that hard times come to an end, that light follows dark, that her name symbolises one of the most important human abilities to carry on. She wondered how much Hope had changed over the last few months, what she would look like now. With any luck she'd enjoy turning the pages of the book and looking at the bright images for now, until she was older. She was under no illusion that the book would ever help Hope very much, but it was her way of helping her, just a little bit.

The story had always resonated with Sister Veronica, she'd often thought how nice it would be to leave all worldly troubles behind and float away with a boatful of animals. The only downside was that they'd make a terrible mess, of course. And the dove at the end of the tale who bought Noah a sign that the flood was receding was a lovely symbol of peace and indeed – Hope. It was a tale that symbolised the rise of new life after a bad and destructive time, and the rewards that could happen if one put one's trust in the universe, God, love – or whatever you wanted to call it – during times of adversity. As the story meant so much to her, she did hope that the child would find some sort of meaning in it as she grew older and understood life more.

Now, she stood and looked at the front door of the pretty, white terraced house in Shepton Mallet, a town not far from Glastonbury. But far enough, she thought, for a fresh start. A new chapter. Pots containing ferns stood either side of the door, and a pretty wind chime dangled in the window. Perfect, she thought. And well taken care of. That's a good sign. She knocked.

'Sister,' Lucan exclaimed as he opened the door, a beautiful wriggling little girl in his arms, her wavy auburn hair now ear length. She was dressed in a pink-and-white spotted top and white leggings, a fluffy bunny toy under one arm. 'How lovely to see you. Come in.'

Minutes later, Hope – now called Asha Hope, Lucan said, as it's what her mother would have wanted – was pulling herself up into a standing position using Sister Veronica's knee as a sturdy aid. They were in the little living room at the front of the house. It had a cottagey feel, with old exposed beams above them, a wood burner in the hearth, and a comfortable – if a little worn – furniture suite. A box of Asha's toys – the brightly coloured playthings overflowing on to the floor – was next to the sofa she'd gratefully sunk into. *Yes*, Sister Veronica thought approvingly. *This is just the place for her to be brought up in; a lovely, warm-feeling home. Oh, I am glad things have turned out like this.*

'Did you know that Asha means hope in Sanskrit?' Lucan

asked, as he placed a steaming cup of tea on a table near her, making sure it was far enough away from the baby's grasp. 'It seems that you and Mona, were thinking along the same lines when you named her.'

'Does it really?' Sister Veronica said. 'Well, well, well. Great minds think alike, as they say, and Asha is a pretty name. Her mother obviously loved her very much, bless her soul. But I can see she has a wonderful, stable life with you now, Lucan.'

'Yes, thanks to you.' Lucan smiled, easing himself into an armchair slowly. He was still somewhat hampered by his injuries, Sister Veronica observed, walked with a slight limp, and he had lost a lot of weight, looked a bit older. But all in all, his recovery was remarkable. And he'd cut his hair. The shorter style suited him. And it was touching to see the utter love that shone from his face when he looked at his daughter. 'I'll never forget what you did for Asha and I, Sister. It was your hard work and your care of my child that finally united us. You are welcome here any time. Truly.'

'Thank you, Lucan.' Sister Veronica stroked Asha Hope's hair. 'That means a huge amount to me. Although I'm still so sorry Hope – sorry – Asha went missing that night from the café. I don't think my heart will ever quite recover from the shock, and I'm not sure I'll ever properly forgive myself for being so careless.'

'That was Celeste's fault, not yours, Sister,' Lucan said, his smile disappearing for a moment. 'Please don't be hard on yourself because of it. She was hell-bent on having everything she wanted, but she was too screwed up by Art and New Avalon to do it in a healthy way. If she'd applied for custody of Asha through the right channels, and proved she could be a good mother and provide a nice home she might well have been in with a chance of adopting her as her own. That is, if what she'd done to Mona had never come out.'

'Yes,' Sister Veronica mused. 'But thank goodness it did. Your cult – do you mind if I call it a cult?'

'No.' Lucan shook his head. 'That's what it really was, I think. Although it's taking me time to work through everything, sort it out in my head. I was there such a long time and that place muddled my thinking. I was told to believe certain things, like everyone else outside the cult being bad people, and the fact that I'd go to hell if I ever disobeyed Art, that it's taking me some time to reorder my thoughts, make sense of it all, if you know what I mean? I understand it all logically, but feeling it seems to be a different matter. But I know how Art ran New Avalon, how he treated people and acted, was very wrong.'

'Yes it was,' Sister Veronica went on. 'I'm glad you can see that, Lucan. Your cult, and Celeste's mother dying, and her sister leaving, and Art abusing her for years, had muddled her mind to the point where all her ethics and morals were topsy-turvy and back to front. Much of that was not her fault, of course, and she was never able to take a step back and think about New Avalon from another perspective like you are able to. But she still had a choice, and she chose to treat Mona in the most inhumane way. There was no love left at all in her at the end. Not for her sister, anyway. It's all very sad, really. Although what I just can't understand is why Morgana tried to kill Celeste. I mean, what was she trying to gain from it? Maybe she was mad?'

'Morgana was trying to gain Art,' Lucan said with a wry smile. 'She was absolutely head over heels in love with him, any idiot with half a brain could see that. She hung off his every word, followed him around like a puppy, did anything he asked. She must have been really jealous of Celeste, seen her as a love rival. It's pathetic really. And Art encouraged Morgana's behaviour, always throwing her enough signs to keep her interested, but really Celeste was his true passion. Always has been. Well, her and Mona. I don't think Morgana was his type, but he found her brains useful so he used her.'

'It sounds like he saw people as objects, there to satisfy his own needs, rather than human beings with their own rights,' Sister Veronica said. 'He was punitive rather than caring, nothing anyone did would ever really have been good enough for him because he didn't want that. He wanted control. And Mona tried to escape him, tried to find herself a better, free life. She was very brave, really.'

'Yes,' Lucan said quietly. 'You're right. Poor Mona. A part of me will love her forever, you know. And it makes me sad that Asha will grow up without knowing her mother. But I have to concentrate on being thankful for what we do have, Asha and I, for the fact that we have each other and a new chance at life now.'

They sat in silence together, watching the little girl throw her building blocks all over the floor, while laughing delightedly at her own game.

'I hear Morgana's finally been caught,' Lucan said a few moments later. 'I read that article your friend wrote about it all. She writes well, she must be a very successful journalist. She presented everything with such understanding, not like some writers would have done. And it was on the front page of the newspaper, pride of place.'

'Melissa?' Sister Veronica said. 'Yes, she's a very fine reporter. And she's just found out she's expecting her first child with her partner Chris, they're both absolutely over the moon about it. She says cuddling Asha gave her some good pre-parenting lessons. She also says she's never eaten so much pickled onion in her life, it's her only craving. And the best part of it is that she's finally given up smoking once and for all.' Talking about Melissa made a sliver of pain prickle at her insides. They'd made up, of course, after their horrific time in Glastonbury, the two friends.

But things weren't the same between them, not yet. It was as though the trauma and stress had wedged an unspeakable block between them, that had remained even after Asha was found. In time, she hoped, that would ease and filter away, but for now she was giving Melissa some space to enjoy her baby news with Chris.

'That's wonderful news.' Lucan smiled.

'Melissa said Morgana was picked up trying to leave our shores on a ferry bound for Amsterdam,' Sister Veronica said, leaning forward to pick up Asha who was stretching her arms out to her. 'I'm so glad they caught her. I was beginning to worry they never would, as she managed to evade the authorities for ages. She was free for so long she must have thought she was invincible. Thank you, that's a lovely red block.'

Asha grinned, showing off five little teeth.

'I hope that woman never gets out of prison.' Lucan shivered. He picked up his mug of tea and took a sip. 'She's a danger, almost worse than Art, if that's possible. At least he passionately believed in his delusions. Morgana isn't mad. She's just evil and devious and prepared to do absolutely anything to get her own way. I can't believe I actually thought she was nice, I used to really like and trust her. She sometimes seemed so motherly and caring. The younger ones called her Auntie Morgs. More like Murderous Auntie from Hell.'

'But that's the way with psychopathic people, isn't it?' Sister Veronica put Asha gently back down on the floor. 'They are good at charming people, but they have no conscience when it comes to hurting them. It's a shame Art died. I thought it would be good for him to face some responsibility for what he'd done. Perhaps he's doing that in the next realm instead. Perhaps people always have to take responsibility for their actions in the end, one way or another.'

'At least he lived long enough for the police to arrest and

charge him,' Lucan said. 'Although knowing Art as I do, he would never be one for admitting he'd done anything wrong. He was absolutely convinced his voice was God, that the powers that be spoke through him. If he'd lived, he'd have found another way to kill himself in the end, I'm sure of it. You know it's funny, Sister. I spent a long time researching the first, proper King Arthur – whoever he was – because I was so enthralled with New Avalon for ages and I wanted to know everything about the history behind it. And I came to the conclusion that Art was much more like Sir Thomas Malory, who wrote the book *Le Morte d'Arthur* – that contains the popular Arthurian legend that everybody now knows – than the legendary king himself.'

'Oh?' Sister Veronica said. 'How so?'

'Thomas Malory was a nasty piece of work,' Lucan said, shifting position, trying to get comfortable. 'He actually wrote the book in the fifteenth century when he was being held in the Tower of London on charges including theft, murder and rape. It always struck me as odd that such an immoral criminal could write a tale based round a highly moral, ethical person. I eventually saw – towards the end of my time at New Avalon – that Art was more like Malory rather than his hero King Arthur. Because Art was a criminal, too, who idolised the principles of the legendary king and tried to personify them. But he never could, because his heart and mind worked in devious, manipulative ways. And he prized his own gains over the needs of other people. And you can't be a truly moral person if you choose to treat people like that.'

'Now that is interesting.' Sister Veronica nodded. 'And he used that moral persona to trick his followers into believing he was really a good leader who would look after them and save their souls.'

'Yes,' Lucan said. 'But the thing is, Sister, Art *really* believed he was King Arthur. You could see it in his eyes. He'd spent so long saying it that he truly believed he was. Isn't that strange?'

'I suspect that if he'd remained alive, doctors would have diagnosed him with some sort of mental illness.' Sister Veronica picked up her mug. 'I don't know much about that sort of thing, but his delusions sound rather psychotic to me. He seemed to go on about being King Arthur a lot, and from what you've told me, about saving his people, without actually ever having anything to show for it. It was all in his head. And he used it to control people. Of course, the tragic thing is that people who choose to join a cult like Art's contribute to the leader's megalomania without realising it, because by choosing to follow someone else's doctrine they've willingly given up their ability to think independently. It adds fuel to the fire, if you'll excuse the metaphor. But of course, ultimately, the choice to carry out the abuse was Art's.' *Although isn't that what we ask Catholics to do in our church?* she asked herself quietly. *Give up their own thoughts and follow our dogma? Is it ever all right to encourage people to lose their autonomy and ability to think for themselves? I still hold that listening to your own thoughts is best, when it comes down to it. Follow your own truth, especially when everyone around you seems to have gone mad. Although I'd never tell Mother Superior that, she'd be up every night for a week.*

There had been several meetings, of course, when Sister Veronica had eventually returned to the Convent of the Christian Heart in Soho. Much discussion needed to be had about her choice to take the baby away, and the events leading up to her disappearance. Mother Superior had calmed down after seeing for herself that Hope had been found, had enjoyed using the opportunity to indulge in her own public shows of relief and prayer instead of spending too much time admonishing her rebel nun. Sister Irene had sourly reprimanded Sister Veronica for weeks, overjoyed at the opportunity of having new material to use to humiliate her antagonist at the convent. But Sister Veronica didn't care about what Irene thought; however Christian the woman professed to be, her motives and actions were anything but, and she'd come to think of her as an annoying pustule that never went away but had to be tolerated. The newly appointed diocesan priest, Father Abimbola, had called a meeting with her, and in his quiet way had asked if she really wanted to continue in her role at the convent, or whether she would prefer to move away. Was she really up to London life anymore? he wondered. Would a place in the countryside be better? No, Sister Veronica had vehemently assured him. She was still very much willing and able to continue in her role. The praise for her from Lucan, when he was well enough to write, passed on to Father Abimbola by Mother Superior, had cemented Sister Veronica's future and she'd settled back into Soho life as quietly and inconspicuously as she could.

'Yes, perhaps you're right,' Lucan said. He shook his head slightly. 'It's so sad, really. That I totally respected him at one time. Celeste and Morgana still did, even right at the end. But their views were as twisted as his.'

'And those two – Celeste and Morgana – are the ones accountable for poor Mona's murder.' Sister Veronica took a slurp of her tea. 'Although from what I can gather Morgana was the one who set the actual fire. Their trials are next month, I hear.'

'I hope they both rot in prison forever.' Lucan's mouth was grim. 'They don't deserve freedom now, not after what they've done.'

'They're being tried separately, of course,' Sister Veronica said. 'The judge may well be more lenient with Celeste. She's going to be disabled for life now, did you hear? The injuries

Morgana inflicted on her were so terrible she's got a huge amount of nerve damage.'

'Yeah, Morgana's good at that,' Lucan said darkly. 'Ruining people for life. The fact that Gareth's now in a psychiatric hospital is probably a good thing. He might actually get the help he needs for what she and Art did to him over the years, filling his head with so many stupid ideas and putting him under too much pressure.'

'Anyway,' Sister Veronica rubbed her hands together, wanting to lighten the mood before she left, 'the good thing is that you and Asha are safe and well, have the rest of your wonderful lives in front of you.'

'Yes, we do.' Lucan smiled as he gazed at his daughter, now rubbing her hands together like the nun had. 'That's right, Asha, good girl.'

'Have you heard anything about Kay?' Sister Veronica said. 'I was so worried about her. She'd woken up by the time we left Glastonbury, but I never heard anything about her after that.'

'Kay's doing well,' Lucan said. 'Really well. We've, er, got quite close actually, since she came out of hospital. It's amazing how a shared experience can bond you together. And she saved my life. I'll never, ever forget that. She's amazing. She's coming over for dinner later.'

'Oh how marvellous.' Sister Veronica clapped her hands together. 'I do love a happy ending. You and Kay are perfect for each other. Two heroes.'

Lucan laughed.

'And you are our fairy godmother,' he said.

After another cup of tea and many cuddles with Asha, after she'd shown her the pictures in the Noah's Ark story – that Asha had bashed very happily with her fist – it was time for her to go. It was hard leaving the child again, but it was in the happiest of circumstances, all things considered. Her heart felt light again, and it was a wonderful feeling. Asha was doing wonderfully well, and had the loving home she deserved. Lucan was on the mend, and was mentally much stronger than she'd ever seen him. The news about him and Kay becoming close was just the thing, eventually she hoped they'd become a happy family of three. All in good time. And the trauma of Jamie Markham that had dogged her for months had finally been put to rest, with Asha Hope teaching her the value of living in the present, and enjoying the good things in the here and now.

As she made her way back to London, resting her head on the train's window, Sister Veronica's thoughts wandered back to the matter that had been occupying her since yesterday morning.

She'd received an invitation, quite unexpectedly, from her cousin Florence, inviting her to spend Christmas at Chalfield Hall. The old Gothic pile had been in the family for years, and Sister Veronica remembered infrequent visits to it as a child, her parents always dressing her in her Sunday best before their arrival, whispering to her in hushed tones to mind her manners while they were there. Florence had inherited it, of course, as the oldest child of her great grandparent's eldest son. She herself hadn't been there for years, remembered never liking it as a child – it was so dark and cold inside, full of the promise of ghosts and ghouls. A very cold building, inside and out.

She and Florence had been mildly close as children, they were similar ages, and had played together whenever all the cousins met up. But as they'd grown into adulthood they'd drifted apart, as people do, with Sister Veronica entering her order and committing her life to God, and Florence marrying that awful man Giles – who none of the family could stand. From what she remembered, his obnoxious personality filled any room he walked into like a bad smell. What Florence saw in him she never knew, perhaps it was his fat cheque book that was alluring, because in any case, Chalfield Hall was not cheap to run and Giles had been left a hefty inheritance by his parents. A marriage of convenience, rather than love, was not uncommon in Florence's circles.

But there seemed something strange about Florence's invitation. They hadn't spent Christmas together for nearly fifty years, and back then it had been with all the cousins and their parents, and grandparents – a fusty mix of old-fashioned, upper-middle-class Victoriana and the more free-spirited Veronica, whose mother had married below her station – a sentiment never said directly but often implied – after falling in love with a farmer.

Perhaps Florence was ill and wanted to spend her last Christmas with extended family before another was not possible? Perhaps it was her husband who was poorly, and her cousin was lonely and needed someone around to help. The possibilities were endless. Whatever the reason, it was very surprising and strange of Florence to write such a friendly solicitation that sounded as though she and Veronica had been close friends for years, when the truth was that they simply hadn't.

Knowing that any nun with an ounce of common sense would politely decline, citing the busy nature of Christmas at the convent as a very valid reason, Sister Veronica couldn't help mulling over the request. It had intrigued her, rather piquing her interest. Also, she felt a familial tug of duty – what if Florence really needed her help and was too polite to ask outright? Mother Superior would not be happy with her going away again, of course. But as it was now nearly the end of March, Christmas was in nearly nine months' time – the early nature of the invitation being another strange factor about it; good gracious it seemed like the last Yuletide had only just passed – leaving her ample opportunity to become a model nun for those intervening months. She would be as biddable, inconspicuous and devout as humanly possible, while hopefully earning at least a few ounces of Sister Julia's trust back. Enough to negotiate a quick seasonal trip away to family, anyway. She may even have time to finish her crime novel during those quiet months, goodness knows she'd waited long enough for that pleasure.

Hmm, she thought. She'd have to mull the invitation over a bit longer before making a final decision. That would be the sensible course of action. *Don't do anything rash, Veronica*, she told herself. *Weigh up the pros and cons, make the right choice. Great Saints in Heaven, it's not as though you haven't had your ample share of exploits and disturbances recently. A nice, calm Christmas at the convent is just what you need, surely. No distractions, no quests to go on, nothing but quiet prayer and festive contemplation.* She rested her head back and shut her eyes. A faint smile broke across her lips. Because at the back of her mind she already knew what her reply to Florence was going to be.

THE END

ACKNOWLEDGEMENTS

A huge thanks to all those at Bloodhound Books, especially Betsy and Fred Reavley, Ian Skewis, Tara Lyons, Maria Slocombe, and everyone who puts an enormous effort in to helping each book launch and fly.

For the encouragement and chocolate, and for generally being wonderful, thank you to Rich. Also thank you to my mum and friends for their ongoing interest, and for making so many supportive cups of tea. And of course, massive thanks to my three bright sparks, Bethan, Olivia and Ben.

A NOTE FROM THE PUBLISHER

Thank you for reading this book. If you enjoyed it please do consider leaving a review on Amazon to help others find it too.

We hate typos. All of our books have been rigorously edited and proofread, but sometimes mistakes do slip through. If you have spotted a typo, please do let us know and we can get it amended within hours.

info@bloodhoundbooks.com

Printed in Great Britain
by Amazon